10.99

Truth Hurts

Truth Hurts

VALERIE NAPIER

Rev. date: 09/09/2014

To order additional copies of this book, contact:
Xlibris LLC
0-800-056-3182
www.xlibrispublishing.co.uk
Orders@xlibrispublishing.co.uk
663784

Chapter 1

Across the open grave, Bethan Rees studied her daughter being comforted by David Meredith, the world famous opera star. He was Ceri's godfather and she was sobbing quietly on his shoulder whilst he gently stroked her long, dark hair. The irony of this poignant scene struck Beth so forcibly that she was unable to concentrate on the minister's words even though it was her husband, Alun, who was lying there in the cold, damp earth.

She was somewhat aware of the mourners singing 'The Lord is my Shepherd' in Welsh to the tune of 'Crimond' and she could distinctly hear old Nellie Williams attempting the descant, warbling above everybody else as usual. Normally Ceri would have been stifling fits of giggles, but not today: this was her father's funeral. Ceri protested angrily that the old woman was spoiling the sombre occasion - killing the beautiful singing with her awful tremolo voice. Secretly, David agreed with her. Beth could also hear Alun's mother howling, as if she were at The Wailing Wall,

'God should have taken me, not my beautiful son.'

Beth thought, uncharitably, that it was a bit late for that now and although it must have been dreadful for her mother-in-law to bury her youngest son, Beth still couldn't understand why Elsie Rees always had to make a spectacle of her self and be the centre of attention, whatever the occasion. The mini stage show continued as Mrs. Rees attempted to throw herself into the grave on top of the coffin but fortunately, Alun's brother, Tony was at hand to drag her away and chastise her for sheer stupidity. Feeling a little peeved Mrs Rees moved away and then noticed that Ceri was being comforted by David Meredith so she decided to push her way over to them. Ignoring David she stood between the two and grabbed her granddaughter's arm as if marking ownership. Ceri could never understand why *Mamgu* made it so blatantly obvious that she disliked David Meredith because he was such a lovely man. At that moment David caught Beth's eye and moved towards her. She looked so vulnerable, standing there on her own, dry-eyed staring down at the dark oak coffin. David wondered what she was thinking as she mechanically threw in a handful of earth. Beth suddenly became aware of his arm supporting her. When she noticed her mother-in-law staring at them David felt her stiffen. He guided her gently away. As they walked slowly towards the car people offered their condolences. Close family, friends and neighbours were to attend the funeral tea back at the house. Beth was sorry that her Aunty Doreen, who was now in a local care home, wasn't well enough to attend as she had always been so supportive but at least her two children were present. Alun's family would be going home soon afterwards as Mrs Rees, who was in her nineties, wanted to get back to her spoilt, over-dependent dog.

Ceri watched Beth move towards the cemetery gate with David Meredith, thinking that she looked as though she was sleepwalking. She wondered why her mother hadn't broken down at all since it had happened. People said it was to be expected because she was probably still in a state of shock but Ceri thought it was very strange as she herself couldn't stop crying. Her mother suddenly looked very old and extremely tired. Ceri was so glad that Uncle David was there to look after them. She was also grateful that it was he who had come to break the dreadful news and had later driven her home from London. Ceri's mind was in chaos. She desperately wanted it to be all over. She yearned to get back to her life in London – an exciting, happy life where none of this bad stuff was happening. She wanted to scream at the world that it wasn't fair – she hadn't even had time to say goodbye to her father because it was all over by the time she arrived home. Her grandmother shook her from her reverie by insisting that she threw earth on the coffin which distressed Ceri even further.

'What am I going to do without him *Mamgu*?' she moaned. Her grandmother just shook her head and started to cry with her, so in despair Ceri ran down the path towards her mother. She needed a stiff drink but knew there would be nothing except tea in the house at least until the Ebenezer Chapel crowd and *Mamgu* had gone home. Beth persuaded Ceri to get into the waiting car and turned to David whispering,

'See you back at the house.' She hoped to arrive home before the hoard descended. As David Meredith carried on walking towards his own car he was stopped by one of the chapel elders, who was anxious to let him know that everybody was glad to see him back in Cwm Rhedyn.

'It's lovely to be back here, even if it's not the most pleasant of occasions,' David remarked conscious of the fact that even after being away for many years he still felt very much at ease in this his home area, surrounded by his own people – people whom he had grown up with – people who had known him before he became famous – people who had kept his feet firmly on the ground.

'We hoped you were going to sing for us in the Chapel lad,' the old man commented.

'Not really the time or place, David replied. 'Today is not about me.'

'Too right, lad, too right. Terrible tragedy, him dying so sudden and all that. Beth and Ceri *bach* will need all our support now, especially yours.' He turned and walked away and David was left questioning what the old chapel deacon had meant by his last remark. He wondered if he was reading too much into it. It had been a funny old day; a day of confusing thoughts.

Beth was surprised to see that some people had managed to arrive at the house ahead of them. As soon as they entered the hallway she and Ceri listened patiently to the same words repeated over and over again – what a lovely man Alun had been, how he was going to be sorely missed within the community and how his sudden death had been such a shock to everybody. Most members of Beth's choir had managed to have time away from work to support her and they sang a beautiful rendering of Pie Jesus in the service which had moved her to tears. Both Beth and Ceri hugged, kissed, shook hands and forced smiles but they were both extremely tired so they tried to escape for a few moments into the kitchen, where Beth's lifelong friend, Carol was busy putting the finishing touches to the beautiful food ready for serving. Carol owned a first class catering business and had insisted she would take care of the funeral tea, thus taking one problem away from Beth. Unfortunately Mrs Rees (Alun's mother) saw them sneak away and followed them.

'What are you two doing hiding in here? Shouldn't you be in there greeting your guests? She huffed, taking one of the canapés, much to Carol's annoyance. 'That food seems a bit fancy for a funeral doesn't it?'

Carol jumped in quickly, 'Doesn't Alun deserve it?'

She had no ready answer so she turned back to her daughter-in-law, 'And what are your plans now Bethan? What are you going to do with this house - it's much too big for you on your own? I can't see Ceri wanting to come back to Cwm Rhedyn, will you *bach*?' For once Ceri kept quiet.

'I've no immediate plans,' replied Beth somewhat impatiently. 'I'll let you know when I've come to any decisions. Why don't you go through and have a cup of tea with the others. We'll be with you soon.'

'Do you want me to drown in the stuff? Just for you to know, we'll be off home once the rest of them have had something to eat. Mind you I don't think this stuff is going to fill them.'

Beth and Carol glanced at each other, willing each other not to laugh.

'You're welcome to stay another night,' said Beth grudgingly. She wasn't sure how convincing she sounded but at that point she didn't really care. Her mother-in-law replied that she didn't want to outstay her welcome. Beth was relieved to know her in-laws were leaving shortly as she was really feeling the strain. Mrs. Rees went to search for her eldest son Tony, who was as insufferable as his mother. People said that Alun had been very like his father – the father-in-law Beth had never known as he had died before she and Alun had started dating. Beth found Tony's wife, Moira as unbearable as her husband with her snobbish, affected ways and their two thoroughly spoiled children. Fortunately they were both unable to attend the funeral. William, their eldest, was a doctor in Bristol and was apparently too busy to take the day off work and their daughter, Annabel, was travelling the world on her gap year. Ceri chanced to ask her aunt if William was a surgeon yet, seeing that he was so busy.

'Oh you are funny Ceri dear, give him time, give him time,' replied her Aunty Moira with her silly, affected laugh. 'Are you working now Ceri or are you resting as they say in your world?'

Ceri was so glad to be able to say that she was currently in the production of Mama Mia in the Prince of Wales theatre, even though she was only in the chorus. It was her very first West End break.

'You must come to see it if you're up in London. I could possibly get you some tickets.'

'We'll see dear, we'll see. I'm an opera lover myself – not really into musicals and your Uncle Tony, as you know, is a Philistine when it comes to any music,' she said turning away as if dismissing Ceri and went in search of David so that she could dazzle him with her operatic knowledge.

'Old cow,' thought her niece.

Whilst they were all eating and drinking gallons of tea, Ceri decided she'd put on her pleasant act for far too long and badly needed a proper drink, so she slipped quietly into the study where she knew there was some Vodka in the cupboard. She popped the bottle under her jacket and crept upstairs to her bedroom. She sat on the bed amongst her childhood teddy bears, looked at the photograph of her father and herself rock climbing and gulped the clear liquid straight from the bottle feeling its fire heating the back of her throat. She soon became a little woozy but definitely felt a lot calmer and more relaxed. Everything appeared to be slightly fuzzy and she would have probably fallen asleep if she hadn't heard *Mamgu* calling her as if through a gathering mist, announcing that they were about to leave. Ceri knew she would have to go down to say goodbye so she staggered across the landing before attempting to navigate the stairs which proved to be rather tricky. David saw her swaying and weaving her way clumsily down the hallway so he went to warn Beth. By the time Beth arrived at the scene, Mrs Rees was already chastising her granddaughter, telling her that her father would have been thoroughly ashamed of the state she was in. Beth couldn't help herself verbally attacking her mother-in law,

'Do you think Alun would have been proud of the way you acted at the graveside?'

Conversation over, Elsie Rees quickly departed, leaving Beth feeling a little guilty as usual because on being provoked she inevitably said things which she later regretted.

Soon after Alun's family had left, Beth went looking for David as she was very concerned about Ceri and whatever she had been drinking. She had already persuaded her drunken daughter to go back upstairs out of the way of the chapel crowd. David told her not to fret - he'd go up to see Ceri and sort her out. Beth looked so forlorn and on the verge of tears that David put his arm around her shoulder but removed it quickly when he realised one of Beth's cousins was staring at them. He persuaded Beth to go and join Carol in the kitchen. She smiled and nodded at him.

Before he managed to get upstairs to Ceri, people finally persuaded David to sing for them. He obliged by singing a haunting, unaccompanied Welsh folk song called *Hiraeth* sung in the minor key– a song about a yearning or a longing for a person or a place. It had been a good choice as it suited the occasion perfectly. Beth was sitting in the kitchen sipping tea with Carol when she heard David singing. She suddenly burst into floods of tears, not really knowing why. She wasn't certain who or what she was crying for – was it herself? She used the excuse that David's voice always triggered deep emotions within her and made her blubber. Carol said nothing but handed her a piece of kitchen towel and carried on clearing up.

In a while David managed to extricate himself from his adoring audience in order to go upstairs to see his goddaughter. He knocked on the door,

'It's only me Ceri. Just want to make sure you're okay.'

He heard her mumble that it was alright to come in. He noticed the empty vodka bottle on the floor and from the sight of her realised she had drunk most of it. Ceri was very glad it was her Uncle David who had come up to her because he was never judgemental. She told him that she wanted to get back to London - how she could never stay in Cwm Rhedyn, that the place and its people suffocated her. Ceri was certain that he understood because David had moved away from the district many years ago, had lived in beautiful cities all over the world and had never returned except on visits to his family. She then started to cry as she told him she would have to stay at home now to be with her mother but he assured her that Beth would be fine, given time. She then started to become very maudlin and the crying increased to a crescendo of loud, uncontrollable sobs. She threw herself on the bed, pummelling the mattress and shouting that she wanted her Dad, so her godfather put his arms around her, rocked her back and forth and soothed her by singing a lullaby as if she was a small child. She eventually quietened down and fell into an exhausted sleep. David looked at her for a while before covering her with a comforter, closing the door quietly and going downstairs to search for Beth.

He found her in the kitchen and he immediately noticed she had been crying. Although David decided not to mention it he wondered what had been the trigger for the tears. He remarked that Ceri would have the hangover of all hangovers in the morning but was fast asleep for the time being. Beth sighed. She was very worried about her daughter – she didn't seem to be coping at all well with the loss of her father. It was so difficult to know what to do for the best. She hoped she would be able to think a little clearer in the morning after a good night's sleep. Carol and David's support was invaluable. Through the open door they noticed that the mourners were starting to make their way towards the front door so Beth went to say goodbye and thank them for everything. When the last one left, she locked the door with an immense sigh of relief that the day was nearly over. When she returned to the kitchen, David had already opened one of Alun's bottles of wine and was pouring a glassful for Beth, Carol and himself. The three old friends sat around the table for an hour or so reminiscing about past times but nobody mentioned the future. Then David said he'd leave them as Beth looked absolutely exhausted. He was staying with his elderly mother in Carmarthen but felt better leaving Beth knowing that

Carol was going to spend the night with her. Carol had always been such a good friend to both of them and he knew Beth would need her support even more in the coming days. He promised to be back in the morning, before returning to London. Kissing Beth on the forehead he quickly took his leave before saying more than he should.

Carol persuaded her friend to have an early night but guessed that sleep would not come easily. She wondered how Beth was going to cope in the coming weeks and what she would decide to do. There had been so many mistakes over the years; so many deceptions that had led to all kinds of complications. It was too late to sort things out with Alun and many others, who had been affected by the lies, but it was not too late to tell Ceri. Carol knew that Beth was contemplating telling her daughter the truth but Carol was not convinced that Ceri would benefit from such revelations or that she could even cope with the facts. Carol also appreciated that other people's lives would be upset, including her own. Although she was worried about the consequences, she would not try to sway her friend's decision one way or the other. Beth hadn't made her mind up what she was going to do and realised that the day of Alun's funeral was certainly not the time to even think about such things, let alone make unusually weighty decisions. They would have to be put off for the present.

Chapter 2

Beth surprisingly fell into a deep sleep as soon as her head touched the pillow but awoke with a start about three o'clock in the morning – the dreaded hour. She had experienced a very vivid, disturbing dream which had left her in a cold sweat and trembling. She switched on the bedside light and gradually its warm, comforting glow made her feel better. Wrapping the duvet around her shoulders she decided to go downstairs and make herself a cup of tea as she knew if she stayed in bed she would only toss and turn for hours as her thoughts became jumbled. Carol must have heard her, even though she had tried to be as quiet as possible, but as always the squeaky, old floorboards gave the game away. After making the tea they both sat huddled together on the sitting room sofa drinking the hot liquid reminiscing about the past – the good times, the bad times, the fears, the complications and uncertainties. Beth admitted to Carol that she could never move on with her life without disclosing certain matters to her daughter, Ceri. Carol suspected this to be true but made Beth promise to give it a lot of thought as Ceri needed a period to get over the loss of her father and would be very vulnerable for a while. She also told Beth that the revelation would need a lot of courage on her behalf. It was imperative that she found the correct words and the right time. Carol was not convinced that that moment would ever come. She had been such a good friend to

Beth since their schooldays and Beth realised she could never have survived certain times of her life without her. Earlier that year she had sent Carol a birthday card with the sentiment — *'You'll always be my best friend because you know too much.'* It had made Carol laugh but she also recognized the truth of those words.

The two women finally went back to bed at daybreak. Beth eventually woke at half past ten. She couldn't believe she had slept so late into the morning as she was usually such an early riser. Carol brought her some coffee and toast in bed before hurrying off to work with the promise that she would return by early evening. Carol's catering firm was preparing for a prestigious wedding later that week so she was extremely busy. Beth felt vaguely guilty for taking up so much of her friend's time but putting those thoughts aside she decided she aught to get up and face the day so took a quick shower before checking on her wonton daughter. She found Ceri sprawled ungainly across her bed, sound asleep. Before she had time to dress Beth heard the front doorbell ring. She donned her dressing gown hurriedly before running downstairs to answer it.

'Morning, Mrs. Rees.'

It was David. She had not expected him to call that early. Seeing her reaction he asked if it would be better if he went away and came back later.

Of course not,' she told him, laughingly. 'Just let me go upstairs and get dressed.'

'Why bother, I like you just like you are,' he teased, pulling her towards him. It felt safe and comfortable in his arms but she pulled away as she felt an immense wave of guilt wash over her. She could also hear Ceri padding her way towards the bathroom and then rummaging in the wall cabinet, probably looking for some miracle cure for her hangover. Beth went upstairs just to make sure her daughter was alright but found her curled up under the duvet feigning sleep. This was something she used to do as a child when something was troubling her. Beth decided to leave her for the time being, so closed the bedroom door and dressed quickly before joining David downstairs.

He was in the kitchen making a cup of tea. 'How was she?' he asked.

'I'm not really sure. She's probably got a headache and feeling sorry for herself but I sense it's more than that. She definitely didn't want to talk to me and pretended to be asleep. The last time she did that sort of thing was when, Katy Morris's daughter died of meningitis. She was in Ceri's class at school.'

David thought about it for a while and then said it was probably a little premature to analyse her behaviour but suggested that perhaps it would be better for Ceri to return to London sooner rather than later so that she could be amongst her friends. She might find it easier to confide in them. In addition she would be performing in the show twice daily, so her life would be more structured and she would not have too much time to think. Beth was hesitant as she felt her daughter needed a longer spell in the peace and quiet of Cwm Rhedyn to grieve. She had suffered a terrible shock and could do with a longer period at home to come to terms with it. On the other hand Beth could see David's point of view because she knew how much easier it had been for her to burden Carol with her problems rather than confide in her own parents. David suggested they gave Ceri the option so he went upstairs to have a word with his goddaughter. As usual he was able to break through to her where Beth had failed.

A few minutes later he came downstairs announcing that Ceri would prefer to go back to London but was worried about leaving Beth on her own. David said he had assured her that Carol would be keeping a close eye on her mother and would let them know if she needed them. David also offered to postpone his return to the city until the following day so that Ceri could travel with him. He would also check on her whenever he could. Beth was eternally grateful to him as she knew he was on such a tight schedule with his role as Cavaradossi in Puccini's Tosca starting at Covent Garden within a fortnight. They sat at the kitchen table talking easily as only people who know each other really well can. He told her how good it felt to be back home and how much he had enjoyed meeting up with so many old friends in the funeral the previous day. It had given him a taste of normality away from the glitz and glamour of his daily life in the public eye. Beth was surprised to hear him say how good it felt not having the rigours of rehearsals, constant practising and having to be pleasant to his fans day in and day out. She said he'd miss the limelight soon enough if he buried himself back in Cwm Rhedyn but David suddenly seemed dissatisfied with his world. Beth was curious because she had never heard him talk like that before. She wanted to probe a little further but the moment was lost as Ceri came to join them looking extremely dishevelled and the worst for wear. David got up and made her a much needed cup of strong coffee.

'Will you be alright, Mam if I go back to London tomorrow?'

'Of course I will *cariad*. Don't worry about me. I've got heaps to do sorting things out and Carol will be keeping an eye on me. Likewise Uncle David will keep tabs on you so we'll both have our guardian angels to help us through.'

They smiled. David suggested they all go for a walk as the sun had decided to come out but Ceri said she'd rather go back to bed as she definitely needed some more beauty sleep before doing her packing. Beth also had to decline as she had an appointment with Alun's solicitors at midday. David offered to drive her there but Beth decided she'd go alone because she realised that she needed to become independent. He understood so they decided to meet back at the house around half past six when Carol would join them for a take-away meal.

The meeting with her husband's solicitors was straightforward as Alun had always been very meticulous about his affairs. Beth also visited the bank, as she needed to sort out things relating to their joint accounts, so it was late afternoon before she returned home. Opening the front door she called out to Ceri but realised that her daughter must have managed to drag herself out of bed and had gone out somewhere. It was the first time Beth had been alone in the house since Alun's death and it felt very strange. She suddenly felt as though she didn't belong there. She realised that she had never considered it her house from the start but it felt even less so at that moment. Alun had chosen the house. He had loved it from the onset. When they had opened the gate and saw it standing proud at the end of the curved driveway he was in raptures. It was a large, solid stone house with a heavy, imposing front door around which grew a rambling rose – about the only thing Beth found appealing about the place. She thought it looked cold and unwelcoming and was way over their budget but Alun was completely smitten. He thought it the ideal family home with its large garden and plenty of indoor space. Beth didn't argue and let him have his house, even though it was far from being her ideal home and she realised they would struggle to pay for it. It would be his recompense. Alun had had his own way throughout their married life because Beth always felt she was in his debt.

Walking slowly from the hallway to the sitting room she become conscious of how little the house reflected her life and taste. There were so many of Alun's possessions everywhere – golfing trophies, a photograph of him running the London Marathon, a photograph of him and Ceri at Alton Towers. There were his books lining the walls – many relating to history, the subject he taught at the local tertiary college, and so many others depicting his interest in sport, gardening and fine wine. Beth suddenly wondered what on earth she was going to do with all the very special wine in the cellar - with her not really being able to appreciate it. Ceri returned to find her mother staring through the kitchen window at the large, immaculate back garden.

'I'll have to develop green fingers from somewhere,' Beth commented jokingly, as she loathed gardening.

'Just put down some decking and cover areas with gravel and grow flowers in pots,' said Ceri in her usual no-nonsense manner. 'Better that, than let Dad's beautiful work go to rack and ruin.'

Beth told her that she wasn't going to do anything drastic for the time being but thought she'd ask Eric, from down the road, to keep it tidy. He'd probably be glad of the extra cash. Ceri was not very impressed with that idea and told her mother to cast her mind back to the time he was chopping a large branch on a neighbour's tree and sat on the bit he was about to chop off.

'Seriously, Mam he's hopeless.' They both laughed.

Beth changed the subject and asked Ceri if she'd like to take something of her father's back to London. She had expected her to take one of Alun's lovely books, a trophy or a photograph but instead Ceri chose the small, glass millefiori paperweight by Baccarat that always sat on her father's desk in the study. Ceri had accompanied Alun to a local auction and had persuaded him to buy it because it was so pretty. It had sat on his desk ever since and Ceri had always marvelled at its dainty, intricate floral pattern formed from the tiny pieces of glass and Alun had made her look at it more closely so that she could also see the tiny animals hidden away within the pattern. Ceri remembered her father's words as she picked up the heavy piece of glass,

'Remember if and when I die, take care of this because it's something we chose together. It's worth quite a bit of money so remember you're allowed to sell it if you're ever in a fix.' Ceri smiled. It was as if her father was still looking out for her. Beth watched her daughter cradling the piece of glass in her hands as she carried it carefully upstairs as if it was something very precious; mystified as to why she had chosen that particular item.

At that moment David rang to ask whether they wanted Indian or Chinese food. They opted for Indian as Alun never allowed them to eat it in the house because he always complained that the house stank of curry for days. Carol arrived just in time for the feast. They had arranged all the cartons casually on the kitchen table and piled plates and cutlery so that everyone could help themselves.

'Dad wouldn't like this,' commented Ceri feeling guilty knowing that her father would have hated the food and the informal way it was being served. Beth felt like saying that it wasn't his choice now so they could do as they pleased, but of course she didn't. However David jumped in to save the day by saying that it wouldn't hurt just once because everybody was so tired. Ceri seemed to accept that reasoning and for the first time in days ate a decent meal. She then went up to her room to watch television, leaving the three old school friends to finish their meal and companionably share a couple of bottles of wine from the cellar before David announced that he'd better get back to his mother's or she'd lock him out. He kissed both women on the cheek, squeezing Beth's hand as he left. Carol persuaded Beth to let her stay with her for one more night and although Beth protested, she was secretly glad of her friend's company.

David came to fetch Ceri at about nine thirty the following morning, passing Carol on the driveway. As usual she wasn't ready so it gave Beth and David a few minutes on their own to talk. He suggested she take the next month to really think things through and not to act rashly as there was too much at stake. Beth agreed with him. He told her to contact him day or night if she felt that she wasn't able to cope and then promised to be back for a few days at the end of the month to help her execute her decision, whatever it was. He held both her hands pulling her towards him, kissing her gently, not uttering a word. Ceri appeared at the top of the stairs. The pair moved apart. Beth felt tears welling but decided she was definitely not going to cry in front of her daughter; she needed to be strong but when standing on the doorstep waving as the car turned from the drive onto the main road, she let her tears fall freely. Beth realised she was now really on her own.

Chapter 3

Beth didn't want to go back into the house. She had a ridiculous notion that the house was pushing her away. So she sat on the bench for a while, next to the rambling rose which she loved, with its delicate pink flowers and heady scent which wafted towards her. She decided to cut some of the late blooms and take them indoors and place them in the cut-glass rose bowl that had been a wedding present from Aunty Doreen. There was still some coffee left in the percolator which, even though it tasted somewhat stewed, was passably warm. They had used the same coffee percolator for many years. Beth had fancied a new espresso machine or even a cafetiere but Alun did not believe in getting rid of anything which was still in working order. As she sipped the treacle-like liquid she walked slowly from room to room. She was finding it very difficult to settle down to do anything specific. She thought that perhaps she should go into town and do some shopping, but that didn't really appeal because she knew she would probably meet lots of people who would offer their condolences and she felt she couldn't go through that again. She wondered if she should sort some of Alun's clothes so that arrangements could be made for them to go to the local charity shop but decided it was too soon to tackle that job. Eventually she chose to go upstairs and change the beds and wash all the bedclothes that had been used over the funeral period. That was a good decision, as the physical work proved therapeutic, blocking out thoughts of matters praying on her mind. When it was time for lunch, she took her sandwich and pot of yoghurt on a tray and ate them in front of the television, watching the one o'clock news. She couldn't believe that she had no idea what had been going on in the outside world for the past ten days. Everything had centred on her own little universe and nothing else had mattered. People had been killed in earthquakes, fires and wars and she knew nothing about it. It amazed her that one's awareness could diminish so much when in the middle of a personal crisis.

Before she had time to take her dirty dishes to the kitchen, the telephone rang three times in quick succession. Firstly it was Carol checking up on her and apologising that she couldn't visit over the week-end because her catering firm was preparing for the important wedding. Beth assured her that she was fine and would look forward to seeing her on Monday evening when she was less busy. Then Ceri phoned hurriedly (as she had hardly any credit on her mobile phone as usual) just to say they had arrived safely, that she was going back to work the following day and would call again soon. The third call was from David. He just called to say 'hello.' Beth put on a chirpy voice so that he wouldn't worry but David was not deceived by her false cheerfulness. He told her that he'd phone again later in the day when he would have more time for a chat as he was on his way to rehearsals in Covent Garden as they spoke. After all that, Beth felt incredibly weary and decided to do something that was very unusual for her – she would go and lie down and possibly take a nap.

Surprisingly she slept heavily and when she woke it was a quarter to six. She couldn't believe she had been dead to the world for so long. She was suddenly hungry but knew there was hardly any food in the house. The fridge contained one egg, some Stilton cheese (which she didn't fancy) and barely enough milk for a cup of tea. The cupboard looked as if it belonged to Old Mother Hubbard, so she walked down the street to the Fish and Chip shop on the corner and ordered some cod, chips and mushy peas to take out. She felt like a naughty schoolgirl as she ate her food out of the paper it was wrapped in, sitting on the settee in the lounge, watching

Coronation Street – all the things Alun really hated. When David called her later that evening she related what she had done. He laughed and told her she was becoming a rebel in her old age. She added that she was going to take a long soak in the bath before going to bed to read a book she had started before all this had happened. David said he wished he could be there with her. She giggled. He told her he'd call her again the following day and not to worry about Ceri as her friends seemed to be rallying round her. This made Beth feel more at ease.

Beth relaxed in a tub full of fragrant bubbles from her favourite Molton Brown collection, which Ceri had bought her the previous Christmas. When she finally got to bed she didn't feel like reading so she played David's CD of famous arias instead. It wasn't the wisest move because the moment she heard his voice, the tears started flowing and by the time he reached Il Mio Tessoro and La Donne Mobile she was sobbing uncontrollably into her pillow. There were so many times over the years that those two arias had made her weep. She often wondered why she always played them when she felt sad thus making herself feel ten times worse. It was as if it was a compulsion. She decided that she would have to snap out of this gloom so she made her mind up to prepare a 'to do' list for the following day. That would help her get on with things that needed attention instead of wallowing in her misery.

She was up bright and early as usual the following morning and opted to take a trip into Carmarthen, her nearest town. Although she was not planning any major changes to the house in the near future, she thought she'd buy a few accessories to spruce it up. It needed an injection of colour in order to make it feel more homely. She thoroughly enjoyed her shopping spree, primarily because she was looking for things to please herself and no-one else. She found some gorgeous beaded cushions in shades of apricot and russet, which would perk up the dark brown leather three piece suite in the lounge as well as complementing the ridiculous cream carpet and heavy, velvet curtains. She also bought a new duvet set in hot pink and black, which she loved. She knew this would give the bedroom a real lift as she was sick of living with too much beige and brown as she had done for the last thirty plus years. Heady with her purchases she treated herself to a delicious, light lunch in the new coffee shop, which had opened in the shopping precinct. She then returned home.

Beth felt really excited when she saw the differences her meagre purchases had made to the house. It had suddenly been infused with colour and warmth and it made her feel more contented. She decided that she would go into town every week and buy oddments to satisfy her own taste so that the house would at last be hers. The telephone rang.

'I've been ringing you all morning, where on earth have you been Bethan?' demanded Elsie Rees as if her daughter-in law was always supposed to be there when she phoned.

'I went into Carmarthen to buy a few things to brighten up the house.'

'What do you mean? Changing things already are you? I hope you haven't gone for gaudy, bright colours. They can look so cheap. The neutral shades that Alun preferred looked so elegant.'

'Well I like a flash of colour here and there and I have to make the house my own now.'

'You're not wasting your time are you Bethan? He's hardly cold yet. Where's Ceri, can I have a word with her?'

'She went back to London with David. We thought it would be better for her, to be with her friends.'

'We? Who's this we? Why should that Meredith fellow have any say in decisions regarding my granddaughter?'

Beth was finding this conversation very uncomfortable so she made an excuse that there was somebody at the front door.

'You'd better go then and sort out your hectic life. How on earth did you find time for my son and granddaughter in it, I don't know'

Beth stood for a minute in the hallway and actually let out a piercing scream. She used it as her release mechanism because if she had kept those emotions building up within her, she would not be able to control her actions. Beth's feelings towards her mother-in-law, at that moment were nothing short of murderous. She wanted to call David but stopped herself, realising that she couldn't run to him every time something or somebody upset her. In her manic state she rushed upstairs and dragged all Alun's clothes out of the wardrobe, stuffed them into large bin bags and carried them out to the garage until someone could collect them. She should have felt sad but instead the act had a cathartic effect. Beth was about to pour herself a gin and tonic but thought better of it and decided to make some tea instead. As she drank the tea in the kitchen she mused on how quickly life could change. It was less than a fortnight since her husband, Alun, had suffered a massive heart attack right there on the kitchen floor. He was packing to go on a field trip with his sixth formers. The ambulance crew managed to get him to the hospital alive, where he was attached to all sorts of pipes and drips but to no avail. Within two hours he was dead. There was no time for his mother and brother to see him and of course Ceri didn't have the opportunity to say goodbye. Beth was baffled. Alun watched his weight, ate healthily, took plenty of exercise, didn't smoke and drank wine only in moderation. He had insisted on working until he was sixty-five but was planning to retire the following year so that he could pursue some of his dreams such as climbing Kilimanjaro and trekking in the Himalayas. Nobody could fathom how such a fit person could suddenly drop dead of a heart attack. Ludicrously she wondered what he would have made of the new cushions. She knew he would have hated them, especially the beadwork and appliqué – he loathed anything that appeared overly feminine and fussy. Beth realised that was why the house had a cold unwelcoming feel to it; it lacked a woman's touch even though two women had always lived in it. She was determined that she would put that to rights so that she could feel comfortable in her own home for the first time.

David sounded very tired when he phoned later that evening, so Beth didn't mention the trials and tribulations of her day. He told her that some of the cast had wanted him to join them for a meal at a swish restaurant after the performance but he had decided he would prefer his own company so had gone back to his apartment and cooked himself a steak and salad; he was a good cook. It was his way of unwinding after a demanding day. He told Beth that he wasn't able to stand the gruelling schedules as he used to and perhaps the day was approaching when he would have to think of retiring or at least take things easier. It was the second time in a week that Beth had heard him talk that way. She wasn't sure how to react so she teased him,

'You could never survive without the bright lights and the hero worship.' David was silent for a few seconds before explaining that the lights had dimmed over the passing years and he didn't need the adoration of the crowds any more, only the love of one or two very special people.

'You know, Beth, there comes a time when one needs to do some things to suit oneself and no-one else and after the events of the past weeks it makes one take stock of one's life and think about making certain adjustments.'

She knew exactly what he meant but also realized that before any major changes could occur she would have to decide whether or not to tell Ceri the whole story. They said goodnight in a pensive mood, knowing that they would speak again the following day.

Beth couldn't get to sleep. She tried blaming it on the new hot- pink duvet cover but knew that it was nothing so trivial. She recognised that time was passing and she was getting no younger. Thoughts about her own mortality kept niggling her. How would Ceri cope if something happened to her? Beth knew at that moment that she would have to tell Ceri the truth so that her daughter would have somebody to look after her and love her. Beth was aware that she would need to remember all the details from the past –possibly write some notes, because Ceri had to know everything, if she was going to be able to make any sense of it.

When Beth talked to David the following day, she told him of her decision although she was worried how Ceri would react. Perhaps her daughter would never speak to her again but she felt that she had to take that risk. David knew all along what her decision would be. He was secretly worried what effect it would have on his relationship with his goddaughter but knew Beth would never give up on the idea so they agreed they would tell Ceri together when the time felt right – possibly in a few weeks time.

They would only have one chance, so they had to get it right. God only knew what the consequences would be.

When Carol visited, the following Monday, Beth announced her decision. Carol was surprised that it had taken her so little time to make up her mind. She had a feeling that it would come to this but was really worried about the effect on Ceri. Carol was gob-smacked that David was going to be present but Beth was adamant that that was how it was going to be. Carol knew it was a waste of time trying to persuade her friend from doing it because she knew that once Bethan Rees had made up her mind there was no way of turning her. Carol wondered why she needed to do it. Why not leave sleeping dogs lie? She hoped that this was not a selfish move on Beth's part – a way of cleansing her soul. She tried to change the subject and talk of lighter topics, but neither was in the mood for small talk. Carol left that evening with a very troubled mind and a heavy heart. She just couldn't see things working out for the best. When she arrived home she decided to phone David.

'David. I was hoping I'd catch you before you went to bed.'

'Hi, Carol. I presume you've heard then?'

'Yes. I'm a bit concerned. Do you think she's doing the right thing after all this time?'

'I really don't know. Once Beth's decided to do something there's no way of persuading her otherwise as you well know. I do think she's doing it for the best possible reasons but I can't see Ceri accepting the situation. We've all got to be prepared for the fall-out - it's going to impinge on us all'

That night there were three people in three separate beds, tossing and turning, wondering how Beth's revelation would affect them and most of all, what it would do to Ceri.

Chapter 4

The next few weeks passed in a flurry of activity for them all. Beth spent innumerable hours writing to and phoning various individuals and companies to inform them of Alun's death. She then had to settle accounts before closing them and deciding whether to terminate club memberships to wine clubs, Folio Society and the local Golf Club. As the flower beds were starting to resemble a jungle, she did persuade Eric to look after the garden until she decided exactly what she was going to do with it. She emptied bookshelves and sorted out her husband's books. She decided which ones she wanted to keep, she gave some of the others to Alun's closest friend and to the school library, where they would be appreciated – after all she was unlikely to read 'The Mycenaeans or The Babylonians' She also needed some space to display her own books on subjects which interested her. Beth sold some pieces of heavy, sombre furniture, which she had always disliked, (and Ceri definitely didn't want,) at the local auction house and Alun's collection of war memorabilia was sold on E-Bay. She took other less valuable items to the weekly car boot sale held on the local football ground. She had never been to a car boot sale in her life and knew that Alun would have hated to see her go to 'such a common place' but she found the experience immensely enjoyable, and liked the easy camaraderie between the stall holders.

It was a busy time of the year for Carol as she had a lot of wedding receptions booked. Her catering business was going from strength to strength and Carol sometimes wished that she could cut down on her appointments as she was also beginning to feel her age. Being on her feet all day, carrying heavy utensils and the late nights were all taking their toll. She wondered why she kept pushing herself relentlessly as she had no children to inherit the company. Sometimes she thought that she should sell up and take things easier but on the other hand she didn't know what else to do with her life – the business was her baby and she would be lost without it. She occasionally discussed it with Beth and her friend could see that she was worn out by the physical as well as the mental demands of the work. Beth suggested she put a head chef in charge of the actual kitchen so that Carol herself could concentrate on the managerial side. Carol was seriously thinking about it and was trying to iron out the practicalities. She tried to see Beth every few days for a coffee or a meal. The two friends were good for one another. On the surface, Beth was very even tempered, predictable and somewhat conservative in her ways whereas Carol was artistic, impetuous and exciting –but not many people saw the real people underneath those facades. Carol was glad and somewhat surprised, to see that Beth seemed to be coping very well with her new life and embracing the changes. She felt that Beth was actually blossoming and coming out of the shell in which she had been hiding for years.

David was performing twice daily at the Royal Opera House, Covent Garden. His role was particularly demanding at his age so he spent most of his free time, resting. He and Beth spoke on the telephone most days but neither mentioned the important discussion they were about to have with Ceri. David tried to pop over to Kentish Town as often as he could to see if his goddaughter needed anything but there was never anybody at home, so he presumed she was spending a lot of time in the theatre.

Ceri, although very busy in the musical, Mama Mia, had another interest which made demands on her time. She had found a boyfriend. They had been 'an item' for months and things were getting quite serious between them. She hadn't mentioned Matt to her mother as she feared

Beth would feel pushed out and lonely after losing Alun but if she was honest with herself, she wasn't sure how Beth would react to certain issues concerning him. She hadn't told David because she knew he would go straight back and tell her mother. So for the moment, Matt was her lovely secret, whose company she cherished.

One evening when Beth had resigned herself to a 'ready meal,' a glass of wine and an evening of television, the telephone rang. Beth could see from the number that it was Ceri. She thought it was unlike her daughter to call on a Monday night so she immediately believed that something was wrong but found Ceri so excited that she could hardly contain herself.

'Mam, you'll never believe it but I've been made understudy to Tracy Emery, who's playing Sophie. Isn't it the best news ever?'

'How wonderful, *cariad*,' responded her mother. 'It will probably mean that you'll play the part at some time or the other. Oh how fantastic for you!'

'That's the point; Tracy has to go into hospital in two weeks time for a minor operation on her foot, so I'll actually be taking over for a short while soon. Oh Mam, this is what I've been waiting for. I wish Dad was here to share my news.'

'I know love but listen I'll try and get a ticket so that I can come and see you. I'll stay up in London for a few nights – treat myself- find a good hotel and enjoy some pampering. I'll let David know –he'll be so thrilled for you. Speak to you soon.'

Beth looked at her watch and decided that David should have arrived home, so she called him to pass on Ceri's exciting news. Naturally he was delighted and wanted to know if Beth could make it up to London to see the show. She told him she was already on the case. David sounded very disappointed when she said she was going to stay at a hotel rather than in his apartment but Bethan explained that perhaps this was the time to tell Ceri the full story. If they decided to do it, she would prefer they were on neutral territory. David agreed. So without a great deal of forward planning the deed was going to be done.

Beth managed to get a ticket for Ceri's show and was fortunate to get a decent seat but at an astronomical price. Carol had mentioned accompanying her but when she realised that Beth was going to reveal all to Ceri during the visit, she decided to stay at home. Beth had also hoped to see David perform in Tosca but there were no tickets available. Every time David Meredith sang in Covent Garden, it was a sell out. People booked their seats months ahead – he was the one opera star that music lovers around the world would queue for hours and pay over the odds to see perform; he was something very special.

Beth decided to go up to London by train so that she could relax. David met her at Paddington and his chauffeur took them to her hotel in Park Lane. Even though David generally loved his car he detested driving in London so he employed a young Italian called Enrico as his private secretary, handyman and part-time chauffeur. This ensured that he remained calm before rehearsals and performances. When they arrived at the hotel, Beth felt a little out of her comfort zone at first but the staff soon made her feel at ease and of course David was used to staying in five star establishments so she started to relax and enjoy the experience. They ate melt-in-the mouth venison carpaccio, a sea bream creation and a delicious multi flavoured ice cream concoction in the restaurant before getting together with Ceri later in the bar. It was Ceri's first night in her role as Sophie. She was on a high when she met her mother and godfather. The experience had been amazing and she could still hear the applause of the audience ringing in her ears. She was too excited to eat but was persuaded, by the young man behind the bar, to try his own cocktail creation which he instantly named the 'Sophie Special.' It was so delicious that she had to have another and yet another and even one more, which inevitably went straight to her head making her giggly and unstable on her feet. David laughed at her and told Beth not to worry as his chauffeur would take Ceri safely home. David arranged to meet Beth the following afternoon as he had some free time. He said they could do something completely different – a surprise - nothing to do with music. Beth laughed and agreed. He also announced that he had paid for one of the body treatments in the hotel spa for her the following morning.

'You shouldn't have David,' she said feeling a tad guilty.

'Why ever not? It's not often I have the opportunity to spoil you and I really want you to enjoy these few days.'

Beth smiled. Ceri left with David and as Beth stared out of her bedroom window at the twinkling lights of London, she wondered what their future would hold.

The hotel spa was up on the tenth floor from which the views were spectacular. Beth felt nervous as she entered the luxurious suites but once the treatment began she felt both refreshed and relaxed. The experience ended with a massage using oils perfumed with Moroccan roses, their heady perfume transporting Beth into another world. David came to pick her up at the hotel on foot. He had discarded the car and his chauffeur for the day. Beth looked radiant when she emerged from her room and David felt certain that the spa experience had done her some good. He greeted her,

'Well Mrs. Rees, you look wonderful and it's a beautiful day out there so we're going to have some fun and sample the alternative delights of London.' They caught the Tube to Warwick Avenue near the area called Little Venice, from where they caught the waterbus to Regent's Park and visited London Zoo. Beth hadn't been to a zoo since Ceri was a child, so she revelled in the pleasure of it all. Beth loved the new Penguin Beach and David bought her a soft toy of a mother penguin with her baby by which to remember the visit. They ate junk food, which David said was obligatory, and he took a photograph of Beth with ice cream dribbling down her chin. Some people did recognise the opera superstar and he willingly signed autographs for them but they did not encroach on their privacy too much and certainly it didn't spoil their day. As the afternoon drew on, David told Beth that he had a wonderful treat planned for her that evening and told her to wear something special. Enrico would pick her up at seven o'clock. She was intrigued.

Beth's eyes filled with tears when she saw the sign up above the restaurant door – Le Caprice. She remembered the last time she was there in nineteen sixty four, when she was only seventeen. David was attending an interview at the Royal College of Music and Beth was his accompanist for the practical test. She had been invited to go up to London with him and his parents for a couple of nights. After the interview David's parents had treated them to a meal at Le Caprice. Nobody knew anything about the place but it looked very nice. Beth remembered the huge menu cards which were as big as her mother's Woman's Own magazine and the delicious food. She particularly recalled eating fresh strawberries in the middle of November – something unheard of in those days. There had been a quartet playing in the corner and sometime during the meal a young man with a guitar perched himself beside her and sang 'Around the World,' especially for her. Beth had blushed, feeling very gauche and embarrassed because everybody was looking at her and she desperately wanted to hide behind one of the large menu cards. She had spent part of the evening listening to the conversation on a nearby table about how difficult it was finding good quality maids in London since the end of the war. She couldn't believe she was rubbing shoulders with people who actually had servants. It had been such a fantastic experience for the young Welsh girl who had previously not travelled very far from home or encountered such sumptuous eating establishments. She told David that she would like to go there again on her twenty first birthday but that wish never came to pass. The restaurant closed its doors in 1975 and re-opened in 1981 under new management. It had been completely refurbished, with iconic black and white photographs by David Bailey on the walls and a long bar running the whole length of the room. There were no reminders of the old place but to Beth it still felt very special. When they entered they were greeted by the Maitre d'

'Good evening Mr. Meredith, your usual table is ready for you.'

It was only occasionally that Beth caught glimpses of David's world. It still amazed her how famous he was and what a privileged lifestyle he had led for many years. It was so different when he visited Cwm Rhedyn – he was just David with none of the trappings. She felt eyes following them as they crossed the floor and she noticed one or two familiar faces from the pop scene and some television personalities dining there. Beth felt as though the whole thing was surreal but she thoroughly enjoyed her evening and told David, laughingly how she could get used to this indulgent life. He smiled at her and thought how beautiful she looked when she was excited and how her dark eyes danced with glee just like a child's even though she was in her mid sixties. It had been a very special evening and Beth didn't want it to stop. However, David had to be at early rehearsals the following morning and Beth had planned to go shopping with Ceri. In the evening she was attending the performance of Mama Mia so they called it a day but Beth found it very difficult to sleep that night.

Ceri dragged her mother around what felt like a thousand shops before she actually decided on the Karen Millen dress that she liked. Beth bought it for her as a treat and she even stretched to buying her a pair of gorgeous red shoes to match by the same designer. Ceri was thrilled with her purchases. They had a coffee and a sandwich before Ceri had to rush off. Beth told her she'd try to see her after the show. She spent her afternoon relaxing, walking in nearby Hyde Park and just sitting in the sunshine, letting her mind wander and watching the world pass by. She later decided to treat herself to afternoon tea at the hotel, which she felt would be enough food to tide her over until after the show.

Sitting in the theatre, waiting for the curtain to go up, Beth felt very emotional. She longed for her daughter to do well as this was her big opportunity to shine. Beth wondered what Ceri was feeling at that moment – was she sick with nervousness or was she excited, wanting the show to begin? When the performance commenced and Ceri's rich, confident voice filled the auditorium, Beth couldn't help but shed a few tears. Her daughter was fantastic in the role of Sophie. Not only did she have a beautiful voice but she could also act very well. She captured the audience from the moment she appeared on stage. Ceri seemed to love every minute of it especially the standing ovation at the end. Beth was so proud of her and was glad that she had arranged for a bouquet to be sent to her daughter's dressing room. Ceri had cried when she read the wording on the card *'You've done your Father proud. We all love you. Mam xxx.'*

Beth arranged for 'Room Service' to bring her a light supper back at the hotel. She knew David would call her as soon as he could after his performance. Indeed he phoned from his dressing room as he was eager to know how the evening had gone. Beth couldn't contain her excitement and pride as she told David how wonderful Ceri had interpreted her role. David was so pleased. He told Beth that he had read what one of the main critics had written about her earlier in the week after her debut performance.

'I didn't want to tell you before you went to see the show but I'll read it to you now. *We have found a new West End star in the little Welsh girl, Ceri Rees. Not only has she the voice of an angel but she can actually act, which is an added bonus. It was evident that the audience loved her performance as Sophie from the tumultuous applause and standing ovation. Without wishing Tracy Emery any ill we hope Ceri Rees will be allowed to play this part for a long time to come.*

'Oh! How wonderful,' exclaimed Beth. 'Has she seen it?'

'I should think so but I've kept it for her just in case.'

'David.'

'Yes?'

'I've decided to tell her tomorrow. She's coming over to the hotel about seven o' clock as she's got the evening off.'

'So have I so I'll be there although I might as well tell you that I'm not looking forward to it one little bit.'

'I know but it's the only opportunity I'll have before I go back to Cwm Rhedyn on Thursday. I have an appointment with my solicitor. Goodnight David. I'll see you tomorrow.'

'Good night Beth.' He replaced the receiver slowly as troubled thoughts of the following day occupied his mind.

The following morning the telephone rang just as Beth was getting out of the shower. It was David asking if he could join her. He couldn't settle to do anything much as he was worried about the meeting with Ceri that evening. Beth agreed that they may as well worry the day away together. He arrived mid-morning so they had morning coffee in the lounge. They then went up to Beth's room but were like two caged lions pacing round and round so Beth suggested they go out for a walk as the fresh air might do them some good and even though there was a fine drizzle it was preferable to being cooped up indoors. Neither felt like lunch but they drank some tea at about four o'clock. Time dragged so slowly. Beth wanted to get it over with now that she had come thus far. They decided to go to the bar for a drink but then thought the better of it as they hadn't eaten hardly a thing all day. Eventually Ceri came rushing into the foyer, her hair dampened by the rain and her cheeks shining with a rosy glow.

'Hi you two! Are you going to treat me to a fancy meal or what?'

'We'd like you to come up to my room first as I want to have a chat with you before anything else,' Beth said looking very solemn.

Ceri's eyes darted from one to the other trying to read their expressions,' 'This sounds very serious,' she commented, walking behind them towards the lift. Nobody said a word. Once they were inside the room Ceri demanded,

'Okay, what's this all about?'

'Let's sit down first,' said Beth feebly.

'For God's sake Mam, out with it. You're not ill are you?'

'No nothing like that. It's just something I've wanted to tell you for many years but I couldn't when your father was still alive.' Ceri was starting to look very worried.

'Ceri, *cariad*, there's no easy way to say this but Alun was not your real father.'

If Beth had struck her daughter she would not have looked more stunned. She didn't utter a word so Beth carried on.

'Your biological father is David.'

Ceri was shocked into life. 'Don't be so stupid Mam, Uncle David's my godfather.'

'Your mother's telling you the truth, Ceri.'

'You just shut up. You're not my father, how can you be?' She was starting to cry now. Beth tried to put her arm around her but Ceri shook it off. 'Did Dad know this?'

'No.'

'You kidded him all these years? Why Mam? Why?'

'She did it for you but most of all for me, Ceri.' David, realised for the first time that that was the truth of it. Ceri jumped to her feet and searched frantically for her coat.

'I don't want to hear any more of your rubbish. I can't believe you'd want to hurt me like this just when I was so happy. I hate you both. How could you do this to me? How could you have done it to Dad?' With that she stormed out of the hotel room.'

Beth tried to run after her calling her name as she entered the lift but David stopped her.

'Leave her. She needs time to digest what she's just heard. Now the waiting game starts. She'll come back to you when she's good and ready. You'll have to be very patient.'

Beth sat down on the edge of the bed and wept. David put his arms around her and held her close until she was calmer.

Beth looked up at his face and whispered, 'David, please stay with me tonight. I don't want to be here on my own.'

'I hadn't planned to leave,' he said, kissing her gently on her lips.

They slept fitfully that night in each other's arms.

Chapter 5

Beth thought about cancelling her solicitor's appointment and staying in London for a few more days in the hope that she could make some sort of peace with Ceri but David persuaded her to stick to her original plan, thus giving her daughter more time and space to absorb the information which had been hurled at her the previous night. Beth eventually agreed but tried to phone Ceri's mobile once more which went directly to voice mail. She wanted to go over to Ceri's flat but David thought that would be a rash move. In the end Beth was resigned to the fact that she should go home and let the dust settle. David warned her that once Ceri started believing the fact that he was her real father, she would want to ask Beth a whole load of awkward questions, which had to be answered as honestly as possible if she wanted to be reconciled with her daughter. Beth had already been thinking about this and decided she would write her account of the events as they had happened in the form of letters to Ceri. Perhaps her daughter would then have a better understanding of how things were. Ceri would have the option to read them or not. David agreed that it was a good way of doing it. Beth would have the time to choose her words carefully so as to make the process as painless as possible.

'Do you think I've opened Pandora's Box?'

'I really don't know Beth but there's no point in looking back. The deed has been done so we must move forward in the best way possible.'

'Do you think I've lost my,' she hesitated for a moment, 'our daughter?'

'For a little while maybe, but she'll come back when she's ready, I'm sure of it. Give her time.'

David suggested that she write Ceri a text message before leaving just to say she loved her. Hopefully Ceri would contact her mother when she was ready. Beth knew that David needed to be in rehearsals by noon so she made it easier for him to leave by asking him for a lift to the station as her train departed at eleven thirty. They said their proper goodbyes in the hotel room as Beth said she didn't want the whole of London seeing sixty year olds 'snogging' on the platform. David was relieved to see a glimpse of her old sense of humour returning. He had decided not to approach Ceri as he believed it could make matters worse and suggested that perhaps Carol could act as go-between if need be so that they could at least make sure that Ceri was safe and well. They agreed that it seemed like a good idea if Carol was willing.

The train journey seemed endless. Beth had tried to read but even a magazine seemed too demanding in her frame of mind. She decided to take a taxi from the station at Carmarthen to Cwm Rhedyn as she felt she needed to get home as quickly as possible. She wasn't sure why. Possibly she wanted Ceri to know that she was always there for her at Tŷ Cerrig and it would always be her home. Beth felt sure that Ceri would need the security and stability of familiar surroundings when she came to terms with everything.

Carol called on her way home from work to see how things had panned out in London. She could see that Beth was very distressed but agreed with David that Ceri needed time to come to terms with the situation. When Beth asked her to act as mediator, Carol was rather reluctant. As she explained Ceri could also become angry with her once she realised that she had known the whole story over the years and had kept it to herself.

'Let's leave things as they are for a few days and if we find she isn't going to contact you, I'll see what I can do,' suggested Carol.

Beth had to be contented with that. She told Carol that she was going to write out the whole story in letters for Ceri to read if she felt like it. Carol agreed and thought it could also be therapeutic for Beth as it would give her something definite to do. Carol persuaded her friend to come home with her for some supper so the evening sorted itself out. Beth sent David a text message to say she'd arrived home safely, was going to try and have an early night and was missing him already.

David phoned her the following morning just to make sure she was coping. Neither of them had heard anything from Ceri but they realised it was too soon. Beth told him that she was going to spend her mornings writing 'Her Letters' as she called them. David was pleased that she was actually going to do something about it and said he'd call her after his evening performance to see how she was getting on. So a pattern emerged for the next few weeks – Beth spending her mornings writing in Alun's old study (which had been transformed into a cosy, small sitting room with some fashionable new teal curtains, cushions and a table lamp), Carol calling in for a cup of tea and a chat on her way home from work and David phoning every night before going to bed to see how things were progressing. There was still no word from Ceri.

Chapter 6

Beth decided that the letters should be hand written as it would be more personal and the laptop wasn't working anyway. Bizarrely it hadn't worked since Alun's death. It made her think of the wall clock in her grandmother's kitchen which had stopped on the day she died. Beth wondered if computers did the same. Realising that she could not rectify her mistakes as she could on a computer, she provided herself with a good supply of paper and a waste paper bin. Beth was quite keen to get started, so she carried her second cup of coffee into the study with her. (It was still strange to call it her sitting room – probably it would be always referred to as 'The Study'.) She was going to write at the beautiful mahogany, antique desk with its comfortable chair. These were things that she could never sell because Alun had loved them and she could always picture him sitting at the desk just as she was now. In her neat handwriting Beth began to recreate her life on the sheets of paper in front of her.

My darling Ceri,

I do hope you decide to read these letters so that you can see for yourself how things happened. You will probably judge me harshly, and possibly David, but I want you to realise that things were very different then – please try to remember that. It may help you to understand some of our dilemmas.

It started a long time ago – when we were still at school.

Such a long, long time ago thought Beth – nearly fifty years had passed and yet she could recall every detail so clearly.

I had been sitting in the mobile classroom (which passed as our music room) for quite a time that particular morning, waiting for the others to arrive. I must have been very keen, probably because it was the first day of the new Christmas term. I had passed my 'O levels' during the summer and was now set to study for my 'A levels' which I hoped would lead to a place at University in two years time. The piano was open so I sat down and started to play Beethoven's Moonlight Sonata. I had my eyes closed as I could play it from memory. You know how that piece of music transports me into a little world of my own. Suddenly something made me stop. It was strange because I hadn't heard anything specific but somehow I was aware of someone standing behind me, near the door.

'Please don't stop,' said a voice, 'It was absolutely lovely.' I turned round to see the most beautiful person I had ever seen. He was quite amazing. I can actually remember gasping, which made the boy think that he'd frightened me. In actual fact he had literally taken my breath away. I'm not sure how long I sat there staring at him – it was probably only a few seconds but it felt like a lifetime. I just couldn't take my eyes away from his exceptionally handsome face.

'I'm David Meredith, by the way,' he said smiling.

'Yes I guessed that,' I stammered. 'We were expecting you and you do stand out somewhat in a school of six hundred girls.' We laughed and I started to relax a little. I told him my name was Bethan Thomas but my friends called me Beth and that I'd be studying music 'A level' with him and two others and that Mr. Gravel was a brilliant teacher.

'Yes I know. That's why I transferred here from Llandovery College where I was a boarder.' He smiled again and I felt myself blush, as I always did (and still do) when nervous or excited. At that moment It was a bit of both because my stomach flipped and my heart pounded as I continued to watch David Meredith. He was slim back then, slightly taller than the average seventeen year old but his face was anything but average. His dark, wavy hair was thick and glossy and a curl escaped and flopped over his left eye. Wow those eyes! They lit up when he smiled and did the most awful things to my inside.

As she remembered that day, Beth automatically fingered the gold locket, which she always wore around her neck. Inside she had a photograph of her husband Alun and one of her daughter Ceri. Unbeknown to anybody else she also had a photograph of David underneath the one of Alun. It had been taken during that first year. For some reason she decided not to tell Ceri about this.

We had all heard about David Meredith because he had the most fantastic tenor voice and had been winning prizes at all the 'eisteddfodau.' Experts were predicting great things for him. I had seen newspaper photographs of him but they certainly hadn't done him justice. I also knew that his father was a consultant in Singleton Hospital, Swansea although they lived in a very large house on the outskirts of Carmarthen. This was common knowledge as his younger sister, Anita, was in our school.

'How did you manage to get here without being mobbed?' I asked, because having a boy anywhere near our all-girls Grammar School was quite an event.

'Actually I crept round the back of the mobile classroom,' he laughed. 'I felt a little conspicuous – I'm basically a coward. I wish I hadn't disturbed you. You play exceptionally well,' commented David. 'You've got a lovely touch and you obviously feel the music when you're playing. I think you'd make a great accompanist.'

'Always the bridesmaid, never the bride,' I retorted.

'Oh! No. It's very difficult to accompany a singer. Not many people can do it well but I've a feeling that you could. Perhaps you could accompany me sometime?'

'Perhaps I could give it a try,' I answered just as Mr. Gravel, our teacher, came in.

Looking back on those school days Beth realised how unnaturally starved of male company they had been. She remembered how all the girls would rush to the window when somebody mentioned there was a boy passing by. She also recalled with amusement the occasion when they, as sixth formers, were instructed to keep their coats on during a visit to a local boy's school so that the boys couldn't see their feminine forms and get unwholesome ideas. Beth smiled, thinking how ridiculous some of the rules had been but at that time nobody questioned them.

I really enjoyed my music lessons with Mr. Gravel as he was an inspiring teacher. Also David's total dedication rubbed off on me. Of course there was that other small factor – I was totally besotted with David Meredith from the moment we met.

It was a special relationship from the start. We talked easily, firstly about music and then about anything and everything. Before the half-term holiday we had become inseparable. Carol complained that she never saw me – she had been my best friend since primary school. David and I talked, laughed and teased each other and day by day it was becoming more and more difficult to ignore the very strong, magnetic attraction developing between us. I worried at first that our little house behind the shop, which my parents ran, would not be grand enough for him but David was not the type of person who judged people by their background. I was always made more than welcome when I visited their lovely house full of beautiful antiques, which was one of David's father's many interests.

One frosty, crisp, autumn day, as we walked hand in hand down by the river in Cwm Rhedyn, he turned to me, held my cold cheeks in his hands and gently kissed me for the very first time. We stood there for ages, not saying a word, just staring at each other as if we knew we had opened the door onto something that would colour our lives for ever. I laughed nervously before running ahead shouting,

'I'll race you to the iron bridge.' He caught up with me before I reached the bridge and swung me round to face him, kissing my cheeks, my lips, my neck – not gently this time but with an urgency to which I responded. I was completely and utterly lost under his spell.

'Oh Beth,' he said 'I've waited so long to do that. You are a very special person and I know we're only young but I think I've fallen in love with you.'

I couldn't believe my ears. How could this gorgeous, talented person love me? Gingerly I replied, 'I think I love you too.'

I know that this must sound like soppy 'Mills and Boone' stuff to you Ceri but that's how it was in those days. We were very innocent. Love grew slowly and we didn't jump into bed with the first boy we met – it was all about the romance and respect. At that moment, life was very simple for us – just two young people very much in love. I was walking on air and everything was marvellous. Carol teased me incessantly, asking when we were going to name the day and that sort of thing. Of course being so young I imagined myself and David getting married – the service would be in Ebenezer Chapel with all the villagers there to witness it and I'd wear a long, white wedding dress with all the trimmings and then of course we would live happily ever after, probably in Cwm Rhedyn.

One evening, just as I was arriving home my mother, (your Mamgu Elen) stopped me saying she'd like a little word before I went to bed. She warned me not to get too involved with 'that boy' as she called David. She said that she didn't want me to jeopardise my education and my future and In addition I had to realise that David possessed an extraordinary talent and had a very promising career ahead of him. He would probably have to go to London or possibly further afield to further his musical career. Mam was evidently worried that I was going to get hurt. Her warning bothered me for a while but just like the silly young thing that I was, I soon forgot the pep talk - after all David and I were so much in love that nothing else seemed to matter at the time. Music was the centre of our lives and I had started to accompany his singing, on the piano, which gave me immense pleasure. He went to Llanelli twice a week for voice training with Madam Beynon and he spent hours practising but we also found time to do the things normal teenagers did. We loved pop music especially Roy Orbison and I remember we first danced to his song 'Golden Days' which we thought of as 'our song'. I think I've still got a copy of it somewhere in the attic. The Beatles were becoming ever more popular and the sheer genius of their work excited us as musicians. We were quite good at jiving and used to go to the Saturday night dances held in the village hall once a month. I haven't tried doing it for years – I probably wouldn't have enough energy to carry out even the basic moves nowadays let alone the high energy stuff such as jumping up with my legs round David's waist and slipping through his legs. I remember the sixth form dance at school where the boys we invited as partners had to be vetted by the headmistress! David was allowed to come of course and people actually stopped to watch us dance, clapping and cheering – I believe we were quite good at it. We seemed to have an indefinable rapport whatever we did together - so much so that David refused to sing anywhere unless I was at the piano. The chemistry between us was unbelievable.

David won three first prizes in the nineteen sixty-four Royal National Eisteddfod held at Swansea. He won the solo, the folk song and the 'cerdd dant,' in his age group. I wasn't allowed to accompany him as The Eisteddfod had their special accompanists. He wasn't at all happy about that but sadly I realised he didn't really need me in order to succeed. His performances for one so young were outstanding. Important people in the music world were starting to discuss his voice and likening him to Gigli. He was interviewed on a radio programme during the Eisteddfod week and there was a lovely photograph of him in the Western Mail with me in the background. The heading read THREE TIMES LUCKY - A STAR FOR THE FUTURE - I've got the newspaper clip somewhere in a box in the attic. Little doubts troubled me after that week in the Eisteddfod and my mother's words occasionally haunted me. I was so scared that David's exceptional voice was going to force him to go away and leave me. I didn't mention my worries to him as we were having such a good time in Swansea. Carol and I stayed with her aunt in Black Pill whilst David camped out somewhere with his friends. It never entered our heads to stay together - it just wasn't done in those days. Mam said she trusted me so that was enough to keep me on the straight and narrow.

Time passed and on my eighteenth birthday, David was invited over for tea, together with Carol and a couple of school friends. We didn't celebrate our eighteenth birthday in the way you do today - our celebrations were limited to our twenty first. However, it did seem like a special day. Even my father had closed the shop early in order to join us. Mam, bless her had cooked Welsh cakes and an apple tart and my lovely Aunty Doreen had sent Mam some money to buy me a fabulous, chocolate, birthday cake. Probably my parents realised I would be away at college the following year. It was an unusually warm, April afternoon, so we youngsters decided to walk down by the river, (which was by now David's and my special place.) David and I walked a little behind the others and when we reached the 'kissing gate' he pulled a small box from his pocket.

'Happy birthday cariad,' he said. 'I didn't want to give you this in front of the others. I hope you like it and that it will always remind you of me.' I found something ominous in those words but when I opened the box, I dismissed those feelings of foreboding. It was a beautifully crafted marcasite brooch in the form of a treble cleft. I was thrilled with the gift and at that moment he held my hands and looked into my eyes.

'I love you Beth; I know I always will.' The emotion in his voice was so strong that I nearly burst into tears. Fortunately the others had just rounded the corner so they didn't see the very passionate kiss we shared. I still have that brooch in my 'special box' in the attic. We were finding it increasingly difficult to control our emotions. Although we were living in 'The Swinging Sixties' they swung very gently in our neck of the woods. We didn't all rush to get 'The Pill'(as people these days suspected) and then jump into bed with anybody we fancied. In actual fact, most of us girls were terrified of becoming pregnant as being an unmarried mother still held an awful stigma. Your family could be shunned and you could be thrown out of the chapel which brought about further disgrace. Young, pregnant girls had illegal abortions performed in back street houses or they were sent away to have their babies and then the children were put up for adoption with heartbreaking consequences. The last thing we would do was to ask our G.P for the contraceptive pill as they usually knew the family and the risk of parents finding out was too great. So there was no alternative – nice young girls didn't do it. The best contraceptive, so we were told, was the word 'No.' It put an awful strain on relationships.

Fortunately David and I had very little spare time with 'A' Levels looming and his increasing singing schedule which involved me as his accompanist. Those wonderful months passed like a dream. We tried to ignore what would happen in the future – as all lovesick teenagers we lived very much in the present and to hell with everything else. Naturally we had applied for college places and our plan was to go together to The College of Music and Drama in Cardiff. David could plan his career as an opera singer and I would concentrate on the piano and go on to a career in teaching. Carol was also planning to go to the Domestic Science College in Cardiff so the three of us were looking forward to doing lots of things together. It seemed so simple but of course things didn't turn out quite as expected.

Well Ceri, my love, I've spent more time today writing than I had intended to so I'll let you digest this first letter before I write any more.

All my love,

Mam

Somehow Beth had been so engrossed in her writing that she had forgotten that it was way past lunch time. She felt the need to get out of the house for a while so she hurriedly ate a sandwich and found herself walking towards the 'kissing gate' on the way down to the river. She hadn't walked that way for a long, long time but writing the letter to Ceri had brought everything back so clearly. She wasn't sure why she found herself crying – it was probably for lost time.

Carol called for her cup of tea as usual on her way home. Beth gave her a resume of what she had written and they started reminiscing about their schooldays and the very strict rules that they had to adhere to – the wearing of school berets at all times outside school if they were in school uniform and never eating on the street even if they weren't wearing their uniform. They laughed, thinking what children in the twenty first century would have made of it.

David phoned that evening, as Beth knew he would. She told him that she was going to send Ceri the letters one at a time but David didn't think that was a good idea because Ceri, in her present state of mind, would probably rip them up and never read them. He suggested she put them in a box and present them to Ceri when she thought the time was right. He then reported that he had gone round to Ceri's house but there was nobody at home yet again. Beth said she'd been trying to phone her daughter but it still went straight to voice mail. David told her to try not to worry and to carry on writing so that the story would be there for Ceri to read when she was ready.

Beth asked David if he knew she had always carried a photograph of him in her locket.

'What did Alun say about that?' he asked. She told him that he never knew.

'Well as this is 'true confessions,' I've always carried a photograph of you with me everywhere and I was unable to go on stage without having it somewhere on my person. Believe you me you've been in some very strange places!' They both laughed. Beth continued by telling him that she had walked down to the river that afternoon.

'It was as if writing about it propelled me towards the place and when I got there I found myself crying.'

'My poor Beth, I wish I could be there with you now. Never mind I'll be down in a fortnight. Is this writing thing proving too much for you or is it just the worry about Ceri?'

'No, no. I have to do it and in some ways it's sorting out my head but I just wish that Ceri would get in touch. Goodnight *cariad,* speak to you tomorrow.'

'Sweet dreams Beth – make sure I'm in them.'

Chapter 7

Beth wasn't really in the frame of mind for writing the following morning but as she had set herself some targets, she at least sat by the desk as she sipped her tea. She watched the rain lash against the window and the trees near the hedge bend with the force of the wind. The weather certainly did not lighten her mood. She wished Ceri would contact one of them but she knew how stubborn her daughter could be and how much the news of her conception had distressed her. It seemed like weeks since that night in London although it was actually only days. David, although he had said that he was not going to contact Ceri, had actually been round to the house she shared with three other girls a few times but to no avail - Ceri was never there. None of her housemates admitted to knowing her whereabouts although David didn't really believe them. Beth heard the postman push some letters through the letterbox so she thought she may as well read them before starting to write. Perhaps there would be a note from Ceri but to Beth's disappointment there was nothing from her daughter. There was however a lovely letter from her mother's cousin, Alys, who lived in New York, saying how sorry she had been to hear of Alun's death. For a moment Beth stopped what she was doing as she felt a great that wave of guilt pass over her once more. She hadn't even thought about him much over the last few days because of the issues with Ceri— she knew he deserved better than that. She glanced at the photograph of her husband on the mantelpiece, and realised that this man with whom she had lived for over thirty years was never coming back and the realisation that he had died prematurely struck her quite forcibly. Beth pushed herself to return to the rest of the mail which consisted mainly of bills and the usual junk mail which would continue to fill the recycling bin. She then began to write.

My dearest Ceri,

It is so difficult for me to write to you like this when I don't even know where you are or if you are alright. I just have to trust that you are. Back to the story:-

Well the crunch came in the April of our last year in school. David was waiting for me on the school steps as I arrived one morning. He told me he needed to talk to me, so we slipped into the Physics Lab. I was shocked and shaken at what he had to tell me. I thought we would both be going to The College of Music and Drama in Cardiff in the autumn but without my knowledge, Mr. Gravel, our music master, had persuaded David to apply for a place at The Royal College of Music in London. David hadn't told me anything about it as he knew how upset I would be but now there was no option as he had to go to London in three weeks time for an interview and practical audition. I felt the tears running down my cheeks and although he tried to make things easier by saying he hadn't been accepted yet, I knew I would be going to Cardiff on my own come the autumn. I was also secretly hurt that he hadn't told me sooner. He asked me if I would accompany him on the piano for his oral test and naturally I agreed – I could never let him down although I felt my heart was breaking. His parents and sister, Anita, would be coming up to London

with us and we were going to stay two nights in a very
pleasant hotel. This was the occasion when they took us to
eat at The Caprice. Of course I never told you about that but
it was such a wonderful experience.

I knew that my piano playing could make or break him
so I tried to opt out, attempting to persuade him to use the
resident accompanist but he wouldn't hear of it. I'm sure
I was more nervous than David – it was a totally scary
experience but I needn't have worried because he rose to the
occasion as he always did. He gave the performance of a
lifetime and I could see that all the members of the panel were
mesmerised. Very occasionally a person's singing voice
can excite you so much that your whole body bursts with
joy and you find yourself standing up and applauding
automatically. That's what happened to the panel that day
and I suddenly realised that he was no longer 'my David'
but his talent belonged to the wider world. Of course he was
accepted by the college and his family was delighted as was
Mr. Gravel, who had recognised the potential of this young
voice in his care. Although I was happy for David, inwardly
I was devastated because I would be going to Cardiff on
my own, the following October. I felt no joy in the prospect.

We spent every moment possible in each other's company
during those following few months. Our petting (sorry for
using such old fashioned words but that's what we called
it,) became heavier and heavier but I always put the brakes
on when we were likely to go too far. Sometimes I regretted
being so sensible and I actually thought of 'going all the
way.' Foolishly I believed that if I became pregnant, David
would marry me and not go away to London. Fortunately
these ridiculous notions only went round and round in

my silly head. I knew in my heart of hearts that many lives would have been spoilt by such irresponsible actions. Mam knew how much I was hurting and tried to talk to me about giving David a free rein, as stopping him from following his dream would only lead to mutual heartache. Of course she was right, but young people in love can be incredibly selfish.

The hours David and I spent together were becoming more strained with the prospect of our separation constantly on our minds. Somehow we managed to do some work for our 'A Levels' but for me a lot of the joy had gone out of it. We talked constantly of our love for each other, how we were going to stay in touch and what our future would hold. We always believed that somehow we would end up together but life's twists and turns can prove to be very complicated.

Well Ceri, my love, this seems like a good place to break off

All my love

Mam xxx

Beth felt drained after her writing that morning. She felt that re-living some aspects of her life, even so far back revealed that some of the hurt had never gone away. Probably the constant worry about Ceri's whereabouts was also sapping her energy. As always, she tried to shake away the blues by going for a walk to the village shop, even though it was still raining. She bought a couple of magazines which she planned to read, curled up in front of the fire, later that afternoon. As she rounded the corner she met one of her choir members, who suggested they go and have a coffee in the new little cafe that had opened in the village earlier that summer. The two women spent a pleasant hour or so chatting about things in general. This was a nice change for Beth from the constant stresses and strains of her current private life. They discussed Beth's return to the choir as everybody had missed her. Beth had conducted the Cwm Rhedyn and District Choir for over seven years. They had been very successful, winning several competitions during that time and had been privileged to be invited to visit America the previous year where they had sung at various venues to the delight of the Welsh expatriates who loved to hear choirs singing songs from their native Wales. Beth began to think that perhaps it would be wise to get back into her old routine and start living her life once more instead of treading water as she had been since Alun's death. She felt more positive about things when she left the cafe and returned home. As she opened the garden gate she could hear the telephone ringing. She ran up the path to answer it just in case it was Ceri. She couldn't have been more disappointed – it was Elsie Rees, Alun's mother. Before even asking Beth how she was Mrs. Rees began by bombarding her daughter-in-law with questions.

'What's this I hear about Ceri?'

'What exactly have you heard,' asked Beth nervously. Suddenly Beth's stomach started churning. She thought for a second that Elsie Rees had got to know that David Meredith was Ceri's real father and for the first time Beth started to worry about what she had done. She realised how that particular news would distress the old woman. Whatever Beth thought of Elsie Rees, she knew that she idolised her granddaughter. However for the moment at least, she was safe.

'Who's this man she's gone to live with, Bethan?'

'Which man? What on earth are you talking about?'

'Well I thought you of all people would know all about it as you always brag how close you both are.' Elsie Rees never missed a chance to pass snide comments. 'I telephoned the house and one of the girls she lived with, said she'd gone to live with her boyfriend, a Matt O'Connor, some actor or other.'

Beth was flabbergasted. 'You must have got it wrong. Matt O'Connor is one of the leading actors in one of the television soaps – you know the one who plays Gerald in that programme you watch about lawyers, every lunchtime. I didn't know she even had a steady boyfriend.'

'We all have our secrets, don't we, Bethan? That's what I was told anyway. I think you'd better check it out. You can then let me know what's happening.' With that she bade a speedy farewell and left her daughter-in law reeling with the unexpected news. If it was true, Matt was very well known but was about twenty years older than Ceri. Beth didn't know what to do. Carol was working late that evening, catering for a Silver Wedding party and David would be at rehearsals all afternoon. There was only one option left to her – try phoning Ceri's house land-line once more in the hope that one of the girls would answer this time. Beth recognised the voice of the girl who answered but it was evident that she became unforthcoming when she realised she was talking to Ceri's mother. Beth explained how worried she was about her daughter and could Ceri's housemate please enlighten her as to what was going on as she was becoming increasingly concerned. The girl eventually explained that Ceri had indeed gone to live with her boyfriend, Matt O'Connor

'Do you mean THE MATT O'CONNOR?'

'Yes. Isn't it exciting?

'Well I'm not so sure about that. How long has it been going on,' asked Beth?

'Oh ages – it must be nearly a year now.'

'But didn't he only recently leave his wife?'

'You'll have to ask Ceri about that.'

Beth ended the conversation abruptly as she was genuinely at a loss for words. She really couldn't believe her only daughter could be so devious. Why hadn't she mentioned this Matt previously and why on earth had she decided to shack up with him now of all times. She really needed to have a word with David, so she sent him a text message asking him to call her as soon as he could. She then sent him a second text in case he was worried that something dreadful had happened.

Beth paced up and down the room like a caged animal, trying to make sense of everything. The magazines she had bought earlier still lay unread on the coffee table – she just couldn't settle down to do anything so she decided to clean the house from top to bottom. Although Beth didn't particularly like cleaning she believed it was a method for dispelling stress or anger and that day it did prove to do her some good. For one thing she was utterly exhausted after the physical work, so she sat down in front of the fire with a cup of tea. Before the tea had become cold, Beth had dropped off to sleep with her head resting on the padded arm of the large, comfy chair. When she woke it was already dark. Her neck was stiff and she felt rather chilled as the fire had practically gone out. She had just put on a couple of logs when the telephone ran. She knew it was David. Beth didn't give David much opportunity to speak as she poured out the whole story with hardly a pause for breath.

At the end she asked, 'What do you think?'

David was finding it difficult to follow her train of thought and the story sounded so bizarre that he couldn't digest the whole situation. When he had a moment to gather his thoughts he told her that they would have to find Ceri somehow so that they could assess the situation carefully and sensitively. Beth suggested that now was the time to bring in Carol, if she was willing. David agreed. He laughed as he declared that they had one hell of a daughter! That was the first time Beth had heard him refer to Ceri as his child and this acknowledgment made something stir up inside – excitement, emotion – she wasn't sure what it was, but suddenly it felt as if factors that had been out of synch for many years were actually aligning themselves. Beth didn't mention these feelings to David but agreed to have a word with Carol the following day and see what they could come up with. As they said goodnight, David reminded her that whatever happened, she always had him and he loved her more than ever. Beth smiled, thinking that she was a very lucky woman.

Chapter 8

Carol wasn't sure how to react to Beth's news, the following day. On one hand she was glad that Ceri had someone to care about her at this difficult time in her life. On the other she knew that Beth would worry about the age gap and other factors relating to Matt O'Connor's past life.

'You must agree that he's rather dishy, Beth,' commented Carol trying to lighten the situation.

'Exactly – imagine how many others feel the same about him. I'm really worried that Ceri's going to get hurt.'

Carol remarked that Ceri was old enough to work things out for herself and warned Beth not to meddle as she'd certainly not be thanked for it. Carol suggested that on her next couple of days off she'd go up to London and try to find Ceri. Hopefully she'd get to meet this Matt fellow and have something to report back. Beth would only agree to the plan if she could pay for the train fare and Carol's hotel. Carol knew she'd have to go along with that or Beth wouldn't allow her to go. It was decided that David would meet up with her in London so that she had the backing of one parent if instant decisions had to be made. David approved the plan so they would now have to wait until the time was convenient for Carol. The one thing that had given them all some piece of mind was that Ceri was at least alive and well.

Beth couldn't settle down to write that morning. She was annoyed and frustrated because she had hoped to stick to the daily regime she had set herself. Instead, she decided to e-mail the members of the Cwm Rhedyn Choir to see if a meeting could be arranged for the following week at the usual time and place. Beth was glad she had done something positive and was actually starting to look forward to planning the choir's next season. She suddenly remembered that she hadn't answered a letter from the Bristol Welsh Society asking the choir to attend their annual dinner and provide the after-dinner entertainment. So the morning passed quickly sorting out such details. Replies to her e-mail came back very quickly. Everybody seemed pleased that the choir practices were to re-start and Beth felt a certain satisfaction that she was getting her life back on track.

Carol called in for a cup of coffee mid-afternoon, on her way back from the Cash and Carry. She announced that she would be going up to London the following day as it was to be a quiet week at work and she felt she could do with a short break. Beth was glad that it was going to take place sooner rather than later. After Carol left, Beth remembered the magazines she had bought the previous day and was about to curl up in a chair with them when she looked out of the window at the garden – Alun's garden, which was still full of flowers. For some reason she went out and cut a bunch of the purple asters growing near the wall, walked down to the cemetery and placed them on her husband's grave. She stood staring down at the fresh mound of earth wondering what had induced her to do that. The act was definitely not pre-planned. Beth had a weird feeling at that moment; she felt a real need for Alun - probably to sort out Ceri as he always had a way with her. Beth stood there for some time and unexpectedly she felt very sad and lonely. As she walked home she tried to analyse those feelings which were troubling her – she wasn't really lonely because she had David and Carol and in due course no doubt, Ceri but she did feel abandoned. After all it was Alun who had always been there when things were tough. He was the only father Ceri had known until a few days previously. David had only been around for the good times – a couple of birthdays, one or two weddings and the odd special anniversary if his schedule permitted whereas Alun had always been there for herself and Ceri for over thirty years. He was present and supportive during the happy celebrations and the really challenging times. Beth suddenly wondered what it would have been like to live with David for such a long time – their passionate love was always there in the background but had never been tested by the day to day routines, worries and stresses. She suddenly realised she had never admitted these things to herself previously and found her thoughts rather disturbing.

However, Bethan Rees never gave herself the time to wallow in negative thoughts so she shut herself in the study and persuaded herself to write to Ceri.

Cariad,

I've just come back from the cemetery. I saw the asters growing near the back wall and cut some of them to place on your father's grave. Don't think me a hypocrite - I felt a great sense of loss when I was there. Remember Ceri, we were married for a long time and went through a lot together.

Getting back to the story or rather the saga – David tried all ways to persuade me to go to London with him but it wasn't what I wanted and at that moment I felt I couldn't even think about my future as my father was unwell and he was finding work at the shop too much for him. I had to spend that summer holiday helping my mother run the business and I soon realised I couldn't move too far away as Dad's condition was deteriorating quickly. David came over to help whenever he could – he moved some of the heavier stuff for us and assisted my mother with the accounts. I knew my parents were hiding something from me and David realised how worried I was about the situation. Sometime at the beginning of August that year my father was told that he had inoperable cancer. It had apparently started in the bladder but was also invading his lungs and God knows where else. I was devastated and decided to postpone going to college that autumn. My mother, on the surface, was not happy about it but on the other hand I think she was relieved to realise I would be there with her to run the shop and look after my father. Our little village store made just about enough money to keep the three of us but it would have been impossible to pay someone else to run it for us. David told me when we were alone together that I should think very carefully about what I was about to do – it was such a waste to throw away my education and bury myself in Cwm Rhedyn but I was adamant that I would never abandon my parents when they really needed me. So I stayed on to run the shop. Ironically I passed my 'A Levels' with two A's and a C which would have been enough to go to Cardiff as I had planned. David had straight A's and I was so pleased for him because the top grades were so difficult to achieve in those days. Anyway Carol had the grades she needed to go to study Domestic Science in Cardiff so I became conscious of being left in Cwm Rhedyn at the end of the summer without my two best friends. It was at that time my mother's sister moved from Newcastle to Llanelli. She would come to help Mam once a week so that I could have the day off and go to the coffee bar in town where Carol had a holiday job. David would try to join us and the three of us listened to the jukebox playing The Rolling Stones – 'This Could be the Last Time' and The Supremes – 'Baby Love,' over and over again. We would make one cup of espresso coffee last as long as possible. The Italian who owned the place used to shout,

'Mama mia, how do you expect me to make a living when you make a cup of coffee last two hours?' We felt sorry for him so we always bought some of his delicious ice-cream on the way out. The coffee bar used to be where that new kebab place is now.

Aunty Doreen quizzed me a lot about my relationship with David. I'm not sure why – I suppose she realised he would be going off to conquer the world and didn't want me to get hurt. I always convinced her that he was just one in my group of friends. That seemed to satisfy her.

Before the end of the summer, we brought Dad's bed down to the little back parlour as he was finding it increasingly difficult to cope with the steep stairs. As the bathroom was downstairs the move made life a little easier for him. He used to wander through into the shop, on his better days, and sit on the chair in the corner, dressed in the grey overall he always wore in the shop, and greeted his loyal customers as old friends. Even though he was so ill he still worried that 'help your self stores' opening in town would have a detrimental effect on our small country store. You don't remember the shop as it was then with its lovely, polished oak counter, behind which my parents stood serving, helping and chatting to the customers. The little shop sold a bit of everything, from food to knitting wool and screws. On the shelves behind the counter, stood rows of large jars containing sweets. Small children (myself included), used to stand and gaze at them for ages before deciding which to buy with their pennies – aniseed balls, sherbet lemons, dolly mixture or little gems. Mam would weigh out the sweets and pour them into small, white, paper bags to which they would inevitably stick so that we children ended up eating half the paper bag as well. I used to love watching my father cutting the large slabs of cheese with a cheese wire – there were only two types available – red or white. I can remember the musty, wet soil smell of the back store room where the bags of potatoes were stored and weighed out for customers on huge scales- smells can be so evocative. The other smell or rather stink I always connected with the shop was that of asephoetida – supposedly a miracle cure for stomach ailments. It was kept in the loft room above the shop where Dad decanted the liquid into bottles brought in by the customers. It had a dreadful odour and its acrid, bitter stench used to linger in the shop for hours. I couldn't believe that it could do anybody any good. Normally my father used to deliver goods to the sick and elderly twice a week in his van but that soon became impossible. Unfortunately neither my mother nor I could drive so I did my best to deliver as much as I could in the large basket on the front of an ancient bike lurking in the back of the shed. Gwilym Williams, our next door neighbour, took the remainder in his car. People were very kind to us that summer just as they have been during this present, sad period in our lives. I know you never wanted to stay in this area but one thing has to be said about the people of Cwm Rhedyn – they have always come together in an emergency and do their utmost to help when needed.

It was so distressing for us to watch my father getting weaker day by day. My mother had been told that there was nothing that could be done for him and it was only a matter of time. He kept incredibly positive throughout his illness – I'm sure it was a brave act to stop us from worrying but of course it didn't work.

Carol came to say goodbye the second week in September and promised to write from Cardiff every week. She kept her promise for most of that first term but then presumably her life became more interesting and hectic. The next goodbye came a few weeks later - I knew I'd have to face it but I dreaded being in Cwm Rhedyn without David. We both cried and promised that we'd be true to one another and we'd write every other day and telephone whenever it was possible. David's parents were taking him up to London and asked me if I'd like to go with them. I had to decline as my father's condition was worsening and I was afraid to go away even for a night.

Although my mother had hoped to keep my Dad at home, unfortunately towards the end of October he had to go into hospital as he needed specialist treatment to keep him comfortable. Mam or I visited every day - one going to the hospital and the other running the shop. Luckily the local bus coincided with the official visiting times, although Gwilym Williams used to give us a lift whenever he could. As Dad's condition worsened we could go in at any time of the day or night. It was such a strain on both of us but particularly so on Mam. Towards the end Aunty Doreen came over to stay with us. She thought I was miserable because of my father's condition. She didn't realise that David's going away had made matters so much worse. Her being around enabled at least one of us to be with my father constantly and when he passed away early one November morning we were both there to hold his hand and say goodbye. It had been a long, cruel illness and I'm glad your father did not have to suffer in that way, Ceri, but at least we were given the opportunity to prepare for the inevitable - something, my darling, that you didn't get.

I wish you had known your Grandfather – he was a very quiet, reserved man but when he did say something, it was usually worth listening to. I'm not sure how he'd react to the story I'm telling you now. The only thing I do know is that he would deal with it in his usual calm manner although I'm sure he'd find it very difficult to understand and accept.

Neither David nor Carol were allowed time off from college to attend the funeral. They both sent beautiful flowers and lovely letters. Of course I understood but I felt desperately lonely on that cold, windy November day. David telephoned on the night of the funeral. He didn't say much but I knew he wanted to be near me and I would have given anything to bury my head in his sweater, smelling his warm scent and feeling his arms around me. We closed the shop for a few days as a mark of respect and then for a while I had to run the place single handed as Mam couldn't cope. She missed my father so much – I don't think they'd been apart since their marriage soon after the war. Even when she did return to the shop, her heart wasn't in it but she soldiered on as she couldn't afford not to.

Christmas was soon upon us and Aunty Doreen wanted us to go and stay with her and Uncle Harry in Llanelli. I was relieved that my mother decided to stay at home because I needed to spend as much time as possible with David and Carol over the holiday period. I couldn't wait for their homecoming! As we had to stock up the shop for the festivities, I made sure that I kept a few of the speciality goods to one side for our own use. Mam was still a long way from being her old self so I had to make sure that Christmas would be celebrated even if only in a low key way. Aunty Doreen, bless her, still came over once a week so that I could take a day off and Mam always seemed a little brighter after her visits – probably being in the company of someone her own age. I used one of those days to do my Christmas shopping in town. It was easy to buy something for Carol as our tastes were similar but trying to find something special for David was far more difficult. In the end I bought him a small watercolour of Cwm Rhedyn by a local artist, which I thought he could hang on the wall of his room in London. Thinking back, it wasn't a very romantic gift but David loved it and apparently carried it with him wherever he travelled around the world. David bought me some expensive toiletries from Harrods. I felt very pampered, although the sophisticated perfume was probably lost on the good folk of Cwm Rhedyn. Having David around again was fabulous, although we were a little shy of one another when we first met up but before long we couldn't get enough of each other's company once again. Mam and I had a very sombre Christmas lunch – just the two of us but David, Carol, Gwilym Williams, next door, and Edna and Eric Thomas (my parents' best friends,) came over in the evening. We played Monopoly round the kitchen table and we had a power cut so had to use the old oil lamp for light. David and I cooked chestnuts in the fire pan under the grate and Mam opened a bottle of sherry and became quite tipsy and talkative after her second schooner full. Carol and I had our usual Babycham with about three maraschino cherries threaded onto cocktail sticks and David a can of beer – hardly a rave but we enjoyed it. When the electricity came back David, Carol and I went into the back room to play some music and the evening ended with a pile of turkey sandwiches and slices of some special cake that I had stocked in the shop. It had turned out to be a much better day than expected.

Aunty Doreen and Uncle Harry came over on Boxing Day and I went with David to some motor bike scrambling near Carmarthen. I went back to his parents' house for tea. I remember we had dainty sandwiches cut into various shapes and a fantastic chocolate gateau which David's mother had bought from a posh cake shop in Swansea on Christmas Eve. We were left alone after tea so we had time to talk. David wanted to know if I'd done anything about going to college the following September. He evidently still couldn't figure out why I wasn't rearing to go now that there was nothing to stop me. David was ambitious and his career meant everything to him and I was starting to realise that I wasn't and to be honest I was beginning to enjoy running the shop now that Mam was leaving most of the decisions to me. I tried to explain this to David but he just looked at me in disbelief, shaking his head and told me I'd feel differently in time, after getting over the loss of my father. He clearly hadn't understood me at all. I felt a bit hurt but I didn't say anything in case it would spoil our evening but it had anyway because David started bragging about the great life he was having in London and the wonderful people he had met. I think he was trying to make me grasp what I was missing but instead it made me recognise that we wanted different things and were changing as people because of our dissimilar environments. Suddenly I became aware that I could lose David and I started to panic because whatever our differences, I loved him just as much. I felt I wouldn't be able to compete with these clever, interesting people with whom he now mingled and I wouldn't be exciting enough compared with his newly found friends in London. I became very quiet and he realised something was wrong. I explained I was just tired and would be better after a good night's sleep and he accepted the reason without question. So the evening ended prematurely. Aunty Doreen wanted to know where I'd been and for some reason I said I'd been to Carol's house. I'm not sure why I said that but I felt Aunty Doreen didn't like David on whatever grounds. My mother must have wondered why I had lied and was about to contradict me but decided not to for some reason. I hardly slept that night because I was convinced I was going to lose David, my soul mate.

The following day I told Carol what had happened and she made me promise that I would let David know exactly how I was felt. So when he came over that evening I tried to explain how I was contented to stay in Cwm Rhedyn – I didn't need the bright city lights with its bustle and excitement and that I actually enjoyed running the shop. He held me close saying that he wasn't trying to bully me into anything but he was sure that given time I would decide to do something to further my education – I was too bright to bury myself in this backwater. You remind me so much of him. He made me promise, whatever I did, that I kept up my piano playing. I had actually already had a request to become the accompanist for a local choir, which I was going to accept but I didn't mention it to David at that time. I tried to enjoy the remainder of the holiday but there were niggling worries in the back of my mind that inevitably things were going to change between us. He was going back to London by train from Carmarthen and I went to wave him off. Train stations are desperately gloomy places at the best of times and I had to fight back the tears as much as I could so as not to make him sad. David forced a smile and said it wouldn't be long before he'd be home again. To appease me he promised that he would try to return for a week-end about half way through the term. I nodded and waved until I saw the tail end of the train disappearing from view and turned towards the town with a heavy heart – I suspected that David was looking forward to returning to the excitement of his new London life.

I'll leave it there for today, Ceri. I miss you so much,

All my love,

Mamxxx

For some reason writing that particular letter had drained Beth. When David phoned later that evening, she found that she felt annoyed with him. It was as if writing about how she had felt back in the nineteen sixties had made her aware of what a wimp she had been. She never stood up to David as she was so terrified of losing him so she never made her wishes clear.

'What's the matter Beth, darling, you sound very cross? Have I done anything wrong?'

'No not really but you did back then – you never believed in me and what I was doing.'

'Hey, what's brought this about?'

'Just me writing one of my letters to Ceri about the time I decided not to go to college so as to stay in Cwm Rhedyn to run the shop. You could never accept the fact that that's what I wanted.'

'At the time, I must admit I thought you were being ridiculous but that was a long time ago and over the years I have come to appreciated that you did the right thing for you.' He sounded worried. 'Do you forgive me?'

Beth laughed as she said, 'I'll have to think about it.'

They talked about Carol's forthcoming visit to London and their hopes of finding out where their daughter had disappeared to and whether they could somehow be reconciled. Beth was worried that they were pinning too many hopes on what Carol could achieve in such a short time. Only time would tell.

Chapter 9

Beth was on tenterhooks the following morning wondering if Carol's London mission would be successful. She knew she was being silly getting so worked up so early as Carol's train wasn't due to arrive in Paddington until after eleven, so there would definitely be no news until late afternoon at the earliest. She was therefore quite surprised to receive a text message from her friend just after lunch outlining that she had already been to Ceri's old house and one of her housemates had given her a landline telephone number – she would not pass on an address, which Carol thought was fair enough. Beth felt excited but somewhat jittery because she knew there were no guarantees that Ceri would even speak to Carol.

Carol phoned the number she had scribbled on a piece of paper and was startled when a man answered. She presumed it was Matt O'Conner so she tried to hide the childish excitement in her voice by pitching it a little lower, thus conjuring up a sound that Carol herself hardly recognised. She asked the man if she could speak to Ceri as she was Carol Hardy, her godmother and was up in London for a couple of days. Matt announced that Ceri was in rehearsals until four o' clock but Carol was welcome to pop over to see her after that time. Carol took down the address and said she'd be there by around five. She couldn't believe it had been that easy but quickly reminded herself that it was only the first step. However she sent Beth another text message to let her know what was happening. She also contacted David as she had agreed to meet him for dinner that night. It was arranged that she'd keep in touch and they would eat later.

Ceri's new home was in a luxury apartment block in Kensington – Carol was very impressed. After going through umpteen intercom systems she was allowed through the gates and into the building. Ceri lived on the second floor. Carol rang the bell tentatively and was left waiting for a few, seemingly long minutes before Ceri answered the door. She looked pale and washed-out, lacking her usual 'joie de vivre.' She didn't try to hide her displeasure at seeing Carol,

'I suppose they sent you.'

'No I was up in London for a break as it happens and yes, I have let them know that I was coming here to see you – they're both worried sick.'

'Right, now that you've seen me you can clear off.'

Carol was taken aback at Ceri's attitude. She tried to keep calm and asked Ceri in a measured tone if she could come in for a moment, just to have a quick word with her. Ceri was about to turn her away, when Matt appeared and asked Ceri jokingly if she had forgotten her manners and invited Carol in and introduced himself. Ceri was fuming and acted like a spoilt child, stamping down the corridor, refusing to speak and closing herself in the bedroom. Matt apologised for her behaviour but Carol told him not to worry as she had known Ceri from birth and was quite used to her little tantrums. Matt laughed as if excusing a small, stroppy child. He offered Carol a glass of wine and sat opposite her on the elegant, cream, leather sofa. Carol felt herself staring at him like a star-struck school kid – thinking that he was even more handsome in real life than he was on television. He had an easy way about him and drew Carol into conversation effortlessly. After a while Matt excused himself and Carol knew instinctively that he had gone to try and persuade Ceri to join them and indeed before too long they both came back together. Ceri turned to Carol and uttered a sheepish,

'Sorry Aunty Carol,' before sitting close to Matt. Carol wasn't sure how to steer the discussion. She decided to keep the conversation light

– commenting on the beautiful apartment, asking Ceri about her work and describing her own busy week including the important wedding she had catered for over the previous week-end. Ceri wasn't giving much away with her matter of fact, monosyllabic answers. Carol was afraid to push too hard in case she spoiled everything but she tentatively mentioned that Beth was missing her little girl very much. Ceri said she couldn't care less – after all her mother had 'Lover Boy.'

'Ceri!' exclaimed Carol, 'How could you talk about your mother and David like that?'

'Quite easily. You have no idea how much I hate them and what they have done to my father and me. You're not much better because I bet you knew everything that was going on. I'll tell you one thing – I'll never recognise David Meredith as my father. I only had one father and he's dead. I want you to leave now, I'm tired,' she concluded with tears streaming down her face. Matt put his arm around her but when Carol got up to go he walked with her to the door. He said he'd contact Carol the following day after trying to persuade Ceri to see her again. He felt that Ceri should sort out this rift because she really needed her mother at this critical time in her life.

Carol called David from her hotel, cancelling dinner as she needed time on her own in order to think things out. She gave him a resume of the day's events and agreed to catch up with him the following day. She realised that David and Beth had a daughter who was hurting a great deal and it would take a long time and infinite patience for them to work things out. She eventually phoned Beth with the little news she had. Beth naturally wanted to know how Ceri looked – did she seem happy? What was Matt like? She asked so many questions in quick succession that Carol felt it difficult to keep up with her. Carol told Beth not to expect too much too soon but at least it looked likely that she would be seeing Ceri again, the following day. She told Beth not to worry – Ceri was safe and living in luxury with a really dishy guy. Later Carol was concerned that she hadn't mentioned Ceri's pasty complexion and drained look and her antagonism towards the three of them but she consoled herself by thinking it was only natural as Ceri had just been through two major traumas in her life.

David sat in his beautiful, lonely apartment wishing that life could have been different. He thought how lovely it could be with his daughter living nearby but being a rational man he couldn't see them acting 'happy families' in the foreseeable future. Beth felt troubled as she was convinced that Carol wasn't telling her everything so she called David. She explained that she found the treading softly approach very difficult as she liked immediate results, as he well knew. David as always was able to calm her down and made her promise that she would stall her inclination to rush up to London and confront her daughter at least for the time being. After all it was more than likely that Carol would be able to see Ceri again the following day. Although it was after ten o'clock when Beth hung up she needed something to focus on to quell her frustrations so she decided to write Ceri another letter. This made her feel as if she had some sort of connection to her daughter. She threw a couple more logs on the fire in the study as she knew she would probably be there for some time.

Ceri my love,

I wish I could be talking to you face to face but you give me no option other than writing to you like this. The joke is that I'm not even sure you'll read these letters.

Anyway to take you back to my world in nineteen sixty-six: - I had decided to take up the post of accompanist for the local choir because it would get me out of the house to meet people. Being at home with my mother at that time wasn't much fun and I was missing Carol and David of course. Their letters were full of all the new, exciting things they were getting up to whereas I struggled to find anything interesting enough to tell them when I wrote back. After my initial nervousness I began to take pleasure in choir practices and found there were quite a few concerts booked around Saint David's Day and there was some talk of competing at the National Eisteddfod the following summer. So my life developed some sort of structure and I began enjoying myself. As far as the shop was concerned, I realised that I would never be able to compete with the new self-service grocery stores so I would have to think of other ways of maintaining a successful business. I wanted my shop to be special – so special that people would come from afar to Cwm Rhedyn just to visit it. So I spent my free evenings planning. I decided to stock speciality foods that couldn't be easily found elsewhere and let the customers taste them before deciding to buy. I installed a large refrigerator in the back room so as to keep perishable goods fresh. I soon realised that more and more women were going out to work in the area so I believed if I could get somebody who was a really good cook to prepare a 'Dish of the Day,' for us, people could pick up these cooked meals on their way home so as to ensure their families were well fed – you must realise Ceri there were no convenience foods readily available and people were only just starting to own refrigerators and freezers in their homes. So I persuaded Katie Davies who used to be the cook in Plas-yr-Efail to come in every morning and prepare the food in our small, back kitchen – there weren't so many environmental health restrictions in those days. One day she would make steak and kidney pie, another stew with herby dumplings and sometimes a good 'cawl cennin.' We had about ten assorted dishes which meant people could eat something different each week day for a fortnight. People ordered their meals beforehand, leaving their own dishes with us in which to carry the food home. It was so popular that in a very short time we could hardly cope with the demand. We had one of the very first 'Take -Aways' and didn't even know it! Suddenly my letters were full of my exciting ideas for the shop and the activities with the choir. Carol loved what I was doing with the food side and David was really pleased that I was playing the piano again. The hustle and bustle also seemed to be good for Mam. She helped me in the shop when it was really busy or she'd give Katie Davies a hand to do some preparation work in the kitchen. By Easter the shop was doing really well. Mam and I set up a lovely Easter display in the window, full of chocolate eggs, Simnel cakes, bunches of daffodils and fluffy chicks. Another interesting thing happened at that time – Gwilym Williams, our next door neighbour, started coming over to visit Mam, bringing her flowers and staying for tea. He also took her for drives in his car on Sunday afternoons. She seemed to blossom in his presence. They went for walks and laughed a lot – something which my mother didn't usually do. I was a bit concerned that this friendship was developing too soon after my father's death but it was lovely to see Mam so happy. I must admit I did wonder from time to time if they had been more than friends when Dad was still alive but I kept my suspicions to myself, not telling even David. You, Ceri are the first to know what I was thinking.

David didn't manage to come home before Easter but it was lovely to see him when he did. Carol arrived home wearing the first mini dress that Cwm Rhedyn had encountered. Apparently she had bought it at the C&A in Bristol (a popular chain store in those days). Carol had always been a bit of a trend setter and she persuaded me to make a little shift dress for myself from a Simplicity pattern that she'd already used. I wasn't such a good seamstress as her but I could make some passable garments when I tried. I didn't cut it as short as Carol's but it was definitely shorter than I normally wore my clothes. Carol taught me how to bend at the knees when picking something up off the floor and not to bend over so that my knickers would be in sight. She also bought me my first pair of tights because up until then we still wore stockings and suspender belts which were really uncomfortable – the boys liked them though. They called tights 'Passion Killers.' I noticed that David had grown his hair much longer than usual and I had to admit that it suited him and I loved running my fingers through its silkiness. Living in cities was definitely changing both Carol and David and I sometimes felt as if I was being left behind. Fortunately Carol never let that happen. I think it must have been her objective in life to make sure I kept up with the times and didn't get buried alive in Cwm Rhedyn.

I met Mr. Gravel (our old music teacher) sometime during that summer. He asked about David of course although I think he was surprised that we were still an item. He wanted to know what I was doing and although he was sorry that I had not continued with my music in a more formal way he was glad that I had decided to accompany the choir. He said something quite strange to me before we said goodbye.

'Always do what is in your heart Beth. Don't ever try to live other people's dreams.'

I didn't really know what he meant by that until years later.

Although David and I saw each other as often as possible during the summer holidays, it was quite difficult as I was working full-time and David had to attend a summer school for two weeks and some of his college friends came down to stay for a few days and then they went camping to Pembrokeshire for another week. However we kept the National Eisteddfod week sacrosanct. David was competing in the tenor solo between nineteen and twenty five and if he won that he could compete against the other three voices in the prestigious Osborne Roberts competition. I was playing the piano for the choir in a competition for smaller groups and was pleased when they came third which was very commendable for their first attempt. David won the Tenor solo and the Osborn Roberts, Blue Ribbon prize as was expected– it was very exciting. Aunty Doreen helped Mam in the shop that week so I was able to take the time off. She had asked me if I was meeting David that week. I mentioned that we'd probably see each other on the Eisteddfod field and said no more. Again I wondered what she had against David. Mam seemed quite happy with the situation and trusted me so she never asked too many questions. David and I stayed in a lovely guest house - in two single rooms. It was so difficult not to sleep together but I was adamant that I wouldn't do it until we were married – I still believed that it was going to happen. We did however have a very special, lovely time. We felt closer that week than we had since David had gone to London but I knew and feared the time was fast approaching for him to go back again.

During that summer Carol started to take an interest in what I was doing in the shop. She helped me rearrange things and get rid of lines which weren't selling any more. The shop was on the way to becoming a high class, specialist food store which I felt needed a new name. Carol thought of 'Bara Menyn,' which I considered perfect. I put it to Mam and once I had her approval our local carpenter made me a new sign which was hung from a bracket over to the door. I can remember standing on the pavement smiling with pride, hoping my father would have approved.

Saying goodbye to Carol and David at the end of that summer wasn't quite the wrench it had been previously as I was building an interesting life for myself in Cwm Rhedyn. I started to become friends with members of the choir- not in the way Carol and I were friends but a sort of mutual convenience sort of friendships which worked well. Occasionally we went to the dances held in the Barracks in Carmarthen and sometimes we'd go to the coffee bar – remember we were still only nineteen. Both David and Carol were pleased that I was getting out and about a bit because they seemed to be having a whale of a time. It was after that that things started to change but I'll leave that story until the next letter.

All my love

Mam

The fire had burnt down low and there was a distinct chill in the air by the time Beth left the study and went to make some hot chocolate in the hope that it would aid sleep. She couldn't help worrying but she pinned her hopes on Ceri allowing Carol to see her again the following day and perhaps make some progress.

Chapter 10

David called to see Carol at her hotel the following morning, so they had coffee together. During that time Matt O'Connor rang, inviting Carol to join Ceri and himself for lunch at their apartment. Both David and Carol were surprised by the invitation but it made them feel a little more positive. Carol needed to go up to her room to change so David left, promising to contact her later. He also said he'd let Beth know what was happening. Carol wore her smart cream dress with her expensive mock snakeskin shoes as she thought that looking her best would make her feel more confident. Secretly she also wanted to impress Matt O'Connor.

When Carol arrived, Ceri was curled up in an overlarge leather chair making her appear waif-like and vulnerable. Carol wanted to go over and hug her but felt the gesture would not be appreciated. Matt was very attentive to both of them but it was very evident that Ceri wasn't going to welcome her godmother with open arms. Matt had prepared a beautiful salad Nicoise for lunch followed by a scrumptious lemon tart which he confessed had come from the patisserie down the road. He opened a bottle of Entre Deux Mers, a white Bordeaux, which accompanied the meal perfectly. Carol noticed that Ceri ate very little and didn't drink any wine at all. Neither did she speak much – just answering when questioned. Fortunately Matt O'Connor was the perfect host and Carol thought him to be very congenial company. When they had eaten, Matt, to Carol's dismay, said he had to go to rehearsals and would leave them both so that they could have time to talk in private. Ceri looked as if she could to kill him and Carol was panicking as she wasn't sure how to handle the situation. In an attempt to make conversation Carol mentioned how she thought that Matt seemed to be a very nice man to which Ceri answered,

'He is.'

You're lucky to be living in such luxury,' ventured Carol.

'Yes, I know,' was the terse reply.

Carol asked Ceri whether she was feeling alright.

'I'm fine. Why do you ask?'

'Well I thought you looked a little pale and I noticed you didn't have much of an appetite, which isn't like you'

'Are you my mother now? Perhaps I've got two of those as well.'

'Stop it Ceri. I'm here as your friend and if you want to talk about anything I'm here to listen, that's all.'

'Sorry.' Ceri walked up to the large picture window and stood staring at the road below. She appeared agitated as if trying to decide whether to talk to her godmother or not. Carol watched her intently and thought there was something other than her father's death and the revelation that David was her biological father worrying this young woman. Carol dared to ask,

'What is it Ceri? You're not yourself. I know you've had several shocks lately but I feel this is something else. Remember I've known you all your life.'

Ceri didn't say a word but Carol could see tears streaming down her face. This was the cue Carol needed to cross the room and take Ceri in her arms, letting her sob on her shoulder. There was no point in asking any questions until the tears had subsided. Eventually she sat her goddaughter down and told her to explain what was worrying her. Ceri took a deep breath and blurted,

'I'm pregnant.'

'Oh,' said Carol, not sure where to take the discussion next. 'Is that good or bad news?'

'The worst.'

'Why?'

'My career has just started to take off properly and Matt's still married to that bitch who's trying to take him for every penny he's got. He's already got five children and he's paying maintenance for them and I know he doesn't want any more because he told me so' She started to cry again.

'What would you like to do about the baby?' asked Carol.

'I don't know. I feel so ill at the moment that I can't think straight.'

'Surely Matt has realised that something is wrong. Hasn't he sussed out that you could be pregnant? After all he's had three wives who've had his babies.'

'I don't think he was around much when they were expecting and I don't believe he saw much of the children when they were very young. He does meet up with them occasionally now but I sense that he doesn't really like children.'

Carol, holding both of Ceri's hands in hers said in a serious tone, 'Now you listen to me. The first thing you must do is to tell Matt, whatever the consequences. Then you have to contact your mother because you will need all the support you can get, whatever you decide to do. I'll make us both a cup of tea before I go but promise me that you'll tell Matt tonight and I'll come over in the morning before going home. In the meantime I guarantee that I won't say a word to anybody.'

Ceri agreed and surprised Carol by asking, 'Aunty Carol, did you ever want children?'

'Yes, when I first got married but it became evident after I miscarried it wasn't going to happen. I must admit it didn't bother me too much – I didn't become obsessed with it. Then when my marriage broke up I didn't think about it any more because I was so busy building up my business. Anyhow I believe I make a much better aunt than I would a mother. As you know I was very involved with you from the start and the great thing was that I was able to give you back to your mother when you became a pain.'

Ceri smiled. 'Yes you've been a great aunt. Thank you. I'll see you tomorrow.' The two women embraced and Carol walked swiftly towards the tube station deciding on the spur-of-the-moment that some serious retail therapy was needed. Her head was spinning with Ceri's news and she realised she'd have to think of something to tell David and Beth about her visit without actually lying or breaking Ceri's confidence. Carol's mobile phone ran twice as she walked down Oxford Street but she let them go straight to voicemail as she wasn't ready to speak to either of her friends.

In Cwm Rhedyn, Beth was trying to find things to do to take her mind off Carol's meeting with Ceri. In the end she walked down to the Post Office to buy some stamps for imaginary letters. At least she saw a few people to pass the time of day and then the minister's wife invited her in for a cup of coffee which only added to the strains of the day. She asked awkward questions about Ceri and when did Beth expect David Meredith to visit again as it was so nice to catch up with him. Beth always felt there was an ulterior motive to her questions but on the other hand she sensed that perhaps she was becoming rather paranoid. It started to rain on her way home and as always the telephone rang just as she entered the front door. She rushed to answer it thinking it was either Carol or David. To her disappointment it was Mrs Rees, Alun's mother. She wanted to know if Beth knew any more about Ceri's situation and became quite impatient when Beth announced she knew very little more than when they last spoke.

'What does Ceri say for herself? She never answers her phone when I try to call her.'

'Not a lot,' replied Beth truthfully, not wanting the conversation to go in that direction. 'I'm trying not to interfere at the moment. She'll bring him home so that I can meet him when she's good and ready.'

'I can't believe you're so calm about it – you usually get so worked up about everything.'

Beth tried to keep her composure and said that she'd let her know if anything major developed. She then made yet another excuse to get rid of her mother-in-law by saying that she had to rush out to catch the post. Beth smiled to herself when she realised how many excuses she conjured up to get Elsie Rees off the phone. As Beth prepared her evening meal, Carol rang to tell her that Ceri was fine, Matt was the perfect gentleman and host and things seemed to be sorting themselves out slowly with Ceri but naturally it was going to take more time. Beth obviously wanted to know all the details and Carol filled her in as much as possible without divulging the truth. Beth still had the feeling that her friend was not telling her everything but she had to be content for the time being. It would have been so nice to have somebody with her in the large, echoing house to offload her fears. She suddenly missed the comfort of seeing Alun pottering about in the garden or reading his books in the study whilst she cooked dinner for them both. Beth couldn't understand these strange images that kept occupying her thoughts. She could only assume that she needed some company and was pleased to learn that Carol would be returning the following day.

That evening Carol and David arranged to meet for dinner in a small Italian restaurant round the corner from Carol's hotel. David was pleased with the progress she was making with Ceri, based on the limited account she had given him of her visit. They were just finishing their zabaglione when Carol's phone rang – it was Ceri. She was crying uncontrollably and Carol could hardly make sense of what she was saying.

'Ceri, what on earth has happened? Try to speak slowly so that I can understand you.'

'He went ballistic. He called me a conniving little tart and threw the large, blue vase across the room – it broke into smithereens.'

'Are you alright?'

'Yes.'

'Where is he now?'

'I don't know. He told me to get out before he came back.'

'Listen Ceri, don't move. David and I are on our way.'

Ceri screamed, 'I don't want David anywhere near me,' to which Carol replied,

'You haven't much choice, lady.'

David wanted to know what on earth was going on and in between phoning for a taxi and getting her coat Carol brought him up to speed on the day's events. Whilst travelling in the taxi they phoned Beth, telling the distraught mother not to worry or do anything rash as they were on their way to Ceri's apartment to sort things out and would call her again later.

When they entered the apartment, they noticed that Matt had thrown a few more things around the place other than the blue vase – the room was a shambles. After making sure that he hadn't hurt Ceri, David instructed his daughter to pack her things quickly and come with them back to Carol's hotel where they could discuss the situation. Ceri seemed averse to taking instructions from David but Carol urged her to move quickly as they didn't want to be there when Matt returned. Soon they were on their way. They didn't talk much in the taxi – each keeping his or her own counsel. In the hotel room Ceri sat shivering on the bed. Carol put her dressing gown around her goddaughter's shoulders and ordered some sandwiches and hot chocolate from room service. David kept in the background as he didn't want to upset an already delicate situation. Eventually Ceri settled down enough to tell them the story.

Apparently she had moved in with Matt a couple of weeks before her father's death – they had been seeing each other in private for about a year. Ceri had suspected she was pregnant but had pushed it to the back of her mind as she knew that Matt definitely did not want any more children – he wanted their relationship to be fun with no ties – he'd had enough of needy women. By the time Ceri returned to Cwm Rhedyn for her father's funeral she was certain that she was expecting Matt's child. That is why she had tried to get rid of it by drinking the contents of the vodka bottle on the night of the funeral– it hadn't done the trick. Matt didn't suspect anything - he thought she was feeling and acting strangely because of the recent traumas in her life. When she had told him about the baby earlier that evening, his face became a bright red in colour and Ceri thought he was going to hit her. Instead he threw numerous very expensive artefacts at walls ending up breaking them and leaving the debris all over the floor He shouted obscenities at Ceri throughout and she admitted to being very scared – she had never seen that side of him previously. Suddenly Ceri's mobile announced that a text message had arrived. It was from Matt saying he was sorry for the earlier outburst and everything would be fine as long as she didn't tell anyone and she had to get rid of the 'thing' as soon as possible. Ceri couldn't believe what she was reading and started to cry once again. Carol suggested that she send him a message in return stating that she would be going home to Cwm Rhedyn for a few days to sort things out – he could make whatever he liked of the implication. Once that was agreed they telephoned Beth outlining what had happened and that David was free the following day to drive them to Cwm Rhedyn. Beth seemed relieved and asked to speak to her daughter but Carol suggested that it would be better to see her in person when she arrived home. Ceri stayed with Carol in the hotel overnight. Matt didn't contact her again.

The journey to Cwm Rhedyn was very tense and conversation was kept to a minimum. The reunion of mother and daughter was tearful so David and Carol slipped into the kitchen to give them some space. Ceri kept saying how sorry she was but Beth assured her she had nothing to be sorry about and told her that they could have a long talk after she had rested. Ceri seemed grateful that her mother wasn't bombarding her with questions as she normally did and thought that perhaps they could now learn to respect each other's need for privacy and space. Whilst Ceri went to lie down the three friends had the opportunity to discuss the situation. It certainly did not look as if Ceri and Matt O'Connor were going to be playing happy families. They did not know what she was going to do about the baby – they agreed not to pressurise her in any way as it had to be her own decision. Both David and Carol looked towards Beth in the knowledge that she would agree, having been through the same dilemma herself. Carol mentioned that it wouldn't be wise for Ceri to go back to live with Matt but of course if she got rid of the baby it would again have to be her decision. Ceri's room in the house where she had previously lived had been taken up, so there was no going back to live there. Nobody knew what would happen to her career but David had let the director of the show know that Ceri was unwell and would not be returning to work for a few days and he was very understanding. Beth realised that whatever happened, her daughter would not want to stay in Cwm Rhedyn permanently – she had always made that perfectly clear. David came up with the best and most practical solution. Ceri would have to live with him, at least in the short term. After all his apartment had three bedrooms and he could keep an eye on her especially if she was going to keep the baby. They thought it was an excellent solution but recognized that Ceri wouldn't accept the suggestion willingly.

Carol decided to go home as she was really tired after the stressful few days. She also wanted to catch up with her business so that she could plan her schedule for the following week. Left alone, David took Beth in his arms and kissed her gently at first and then more passionately as they realised the hunger for each other had not been satisfied in a long, long time. They were tempted to go upstairs to Beth's bedroom but knew that couldn't happen with their daughter in the house.

'Where shall I be sleeping tonight?' asked David sheepishly.

'It's the spare bedroom for you I'm afraid, my love. We can't risk upsetting Ceri for the time being.'

'Can I tiptoe into your bed in the middle of the night?' he suggested kissing the nape of her neck.

Beth laughed, 'No you can not – I'll have to lock the door.'

So they had to be content with a few stolen kisses and a hug or two and although it was a difficult situation for them they were both willing to do anything to help Ceri through her problems.

Beth took some salmon fillets from the fridge and started preparing a sauce to accompany pasta for their evening meal. She was surprised when David came over to lend a hand as she was not used to a man helping her in the kitchen. Alun could toast some bread and open and heat a tin of baked beans in an emergency but that was the height of his culinary skills. He was of the old world – a woman's place and all that. It hadn't really worried Beth because her father had been just the same, so she was used to it. On the other hand it was lovely to share such routine jobs with somebody. David took over the cooking and Beth set the table and opened the wine. As she went over to the cupboard to fetch the wine glasses, she noticed Ceri standing at the door watching them.

'Very cosy – a tableau of perfect domesticity!'

Beth tried to ignore the snide remark and asked Ceri if she'd be joining them for a meal. Ceri refused using the excuse that she felt like going for a walk in the fresh air but suggested they kept her some in the fridge so that she could heat it up later. In a way Beth was relieved as dinner would be less of a strain without her. David cleared up after the meal and stacked the dishwasher, persuading Beth to go through to the lounge and put her feet up. He eventually came to sit beside her and she snuggled up to him laying her head on his chest, comforted by the reassuring rhythm of his heart. He kissed the top of her head before moving down to her lips. They heard the front door open so they quickly moved apart like silly teenagers. They could hear Ceri moving around in the kitchen and they could hear her re-heating the food in the microwave. Beth switched on the television and they watched an old episode of Bergerac which they actually quite enjoyed, wallowing in the nostalgia. Ceri came in to say goodnight and much to their surprise asked David where he was going to sleep that night.

'In the spare room. Why?' he answered.

'Where would you sleep if I wasn't here – honestly?'

Beth piped up, 'Honestly? – probably with me.' She didn't believe in conjuring any more lies.

Ceri surprised them by saying, 'If that's what you want, just do it. After all who am I to judge anyone?' Beth and David looked at each other incredulously. They couldn't believe that their daughter had just given her permission for them to sleep together. David and Beth had never flaunted their relationship so they decided to keep it that way and sleep in separate bedrooms that night as planned, primarily for Ceri's sake. Also, secretly, Beth would have found the situation uncomfortable as they had never, in the many years they had known each another, made love in Alun's bed.

Ceri smiled to herself when she heard her parents saying goodnight at the top of the stairs and then moving on to their separate bedrooms. At least, thought Ceri, they had enough respect for her and her father to do that. She was glad.

Chapter 11

David had to be back in London by the following afternoon for rehearsals, so he left Cwm Rhedyn shortly after breakfast. Ceri had remained in bed and had not come down to say goodbye to him but nobody made an issue of it. Later, Beth took her up some toast but when she heard her being sick in the bathroom, decided to take it away again. Poor kid, thought Beth – she remembered that stage of pregnancy very well. When Ceri eventually emerged, Beth noticed that she was very pale and had lost some weight and when Ceri admitted to not having seen a doctor, Beth made an appointment for her to see the local GP that same afternoon. It was confirmed that she was eight weeks pregnant and that tallied with Ceri's own calculations. At least it now gave them a definite time-scale to work within. Matt telephoned Ceri early that evening and she came away from the phone in tears. Apparently he had asked her when she was having the termination and when she would be returning to him in London.

'What did you say?' questioned Beth cautiously.

'That I hadn't decided what I was going to do yet.'

'What was his reaction to that?'

'He became really angry again and told me I was being bloody stupid and not to think about coming back to him if I hadn't got rid of it,' replied

Ceri tearfully. Beth cradled her daughter in her arms, telling her not to let Matt or anybody else bully her into doing anything she didn't want to.

'I don't know what to do, Mam,' pleaded Ceri. 'Did you consider getting rid of me?'

'Never,' answered Beth truthfully. David was already married and that sort of scandal could have ruined his career and I still loved him too much to do that. I desperately wanted to keep David's child and your father was the best candidate for the job of being your dad as I was already married to him. I did the only thing I could think of in the circumstances. Ceri didn't say a word but just sat very quietly deep in thought. Beth felt it was the right time to tell Ceri about the letters she had been writing, chronicling her story as honestly as she could from the beginning.

'I hope you'll read them Ceri because then you may be able to understand certain things which need explaining. Ask me any questions relating to them and I shall try to answer them as candidly as I can. Up to now I've written a few – I'll go back to writing more tomorrow, now that I know you're safe. When you're ready, ask me for them.' The subject was then dropped because Carol called in on her way home. She was given a resume of the day's events and Ceri invited her to stay and eat with them, much to Beth's surprise

The next few days passed with Ceri spending most of her time up in her room. Beth thought it was best not to interfere at this stage so she discussed any matters which were troubling her with David on the phone or with Carol, who usually turned up sometime during the day for a coffee and chat. This gave Beth some free time to write more letters to Ceri because she felt it could be important that her daughter read them in the not too distant future. The study was becoming her sanctuary as it had been Alun's previously. It was a small, cosy room with a proper fire and comfy old chairs and Beth found it easier to settle there than in the much larger, impersonal lounge. She had removed some sombre, bronze artefacts, which Alun had admired, and replaced them with a few choice pieces of colourful ceramics and modern soft furnishings but other than that the room had remained more or less the same. After leaving the letter writing for a few days, Beth was finding it difficult to get started again. However she now felt that there was at least some purpose to it so she was encouraged to keep at it.

Dear Ceri

You cannot believe how good it is to be writing this letter knowing that you are safe and we are at least on speaking terms again.

Let me take you back to the first time I sensed that David was seeing somebody else. A certain name kept creeping into his letters. He constantly mentioning how he admired the famous opera star from Spain who was visiting London for a few months before singing in La Scala, Milan. She would be giving master classes to the most promising students, one of which was David. He seemed besotted with her soprano voice and they had even sung a duet together in one of the Proms concerts held in The Royal Albert Hall which was just across the road from The Royal College of Music. It was indeed an accolade and he sent me a newspaper cutting which raved about the two of them' and their extraordinary voices which rose as one to the accompaniment of angels.' Isabella Rodriguez was quite a few years older than David but from all accounts exceptionally beautiful with an abundance of glossy black hair, smooth olive skin and a voluptuous body. I wasn't surprised that David was being lured by this woman. On the other hand he was extremely handsome and any woman would be proud to be seen on his arm - especially an older one. David still wrote to me regularly but the contents changed subtly as time passed- he wasn't so loving – just newsier. He used to ask me to go up to London for a few days again and again but I always made some excuse not to go. Suddenly he stopped asking. It wasn't that I didn't want to be with him but I was worried that I wouldn't fit in with his new friends – I wasn't as gregarious as David and possibly my self-esteem was rather low. I knew something was wrong but I was too scared to confront him with my worries because I was afraid of hearing the truth. I felt I couldn't survive without David. I told Carol how I felt and she suggested I jump on the next train and surprise him. Of course I didn't go and Carol called me a defeatist. To be honest I really don't think it would have made any difference because at that time David was very ambitious and would have done anything to further his career. I couldn't blame him because I realised what a phenomenal talent he had. It would have been too difficult for me to fit into his world at that point. He came home less and less frequently because he was in great demand even though he was still studying at college.

My mother realised there was something wrong so one morning when the shop was quiet, she brought me a cup of tea and sat me down.

'Let him go love,' she said, 'he's following his dream and it would be very foolish to stop him – he'd never thank you for it. Someday he may realise what he really wants, but until then just set him free.' My mother was a very wise woman and always seemed to know what I was thinking. I cried a lot over the next few days but then mustered the courage to write him a letter stating that I had come to the conclusion that we were following very different paths in life and perhaps it would be better for us both if we ended our relationship. I cried as I sealed the envelope and cried even more when I dropped the letter into the post box. I had to wait over a week before he replied - probably it took him that long to decide what he was going to say. He told me that he was finding it really difficult to maintain a long distance liaison especially now that he had so many singing commitments over and above his studies. Of course he said he realised that I also had my work to consider and couldn't just leave the business to travel to London to visit him. He pointed out that we would no doubt meet sometime during the summer holidays and we could talk then. I'll always remember how he ended the letter,

'Take care my beautiful Beth, I will always love you,' which he did in his own way. I often wondered what would have happened if I'd gone up to London. Could I have saved the relationship then? I don't think so and I now know I wouldn't have survived London any more than he could tolerate being permanently in Cwm Rhedyn. I didn't see him at all during that summer but at least Carol was around to boost my morale and make me laugh. She took a great interest in what I was doing in the shop and gave me new suggestions on how to expand my product lines. I liked her ideas - they were fresh and exciting. One day when we were rearranging a window display Carol turned to me and asked,

'How would you feel about me coming into the business with you? I could develop the fresh produce side of it and perhaps expand into catering whilst you could concentrate on the dried goods, the ordering and the accounts. What do you think?'

'But I assumed you were going into teaching after leaving College.'

'I've changed my mind – I want to work with food but not children. I think that between us we could turn this place into a little gold mine.'

It was such a shock that I couldn't immediately think of an answer, so I told her to give me time to consider it. I reflected on the idea for a couple of days. I could find lots of positive points to it and it would be lovely working with Carol on a joint project. Mam wasn't really involved with the shop at all by that time but she did of course own the building. She seemed relatively happy pottering about in her pretty garden, preparing meals for the two of us and going out and about with Gwilym Williams, next door. Katie Davies, who was cooking for the shop, had mentioned that she couldn't carry on working for ever, so that problem would be solved. I had to discuss the plan with Mam before exploring the proposal any further. She thought it was a good idea as long as the business could provide us both with a reasonable income. When Carol came over at the end of that week, we started talking about the future, seriously. It wouldn't happen immediately as Carol needed to finish her College course first but that gave us enough time to plan everything carefully. So when it was time for Carol to go back to Cardiff at the end of the summer, I was left with enough exciting matter to occupy me until I saw her again.

There was also plenty to do in the choir as Christmas approached. We had various concerts booked in the locality and a Christmas service in the village church. I also met a few choir members from time to time and went to a couple of dances with them in town and I even allowed one or two boys to take me home but nothing ever came of the relationships mainly because they weren't my type.

The boys with whom I would have had things in common were away at College or University – the ones that were available were usually farmers' sons and I didn't fit very comfortably into their world and I'm sure their parents would not have thought me much of a catch for their boys. I still secretly longed for David so much. I was really surprised to receive a letter from him just before Christmas saying that he had missed not seeing me over the summer and was not likely to see me over the coming holiday period either as he was performing in a production of Handel's Messiah up in London, spending Christmas with his uncle and aunt in Surrey (apparently his parents and sister would be joining him there) and then he was off to Spain for a short break before the College term re-started, and I could guess who he was going to see there. I was baffled as to why he had written to me – it was if he wanted my seal of approval; indeed I wished he hadn't contacted me because I became unsettled all over again and Mam was very annoyed with him for upsetting me. However, the shop was very busy towards Christmas and the displays I had created made it look like an enchanting, winter wonderland. The customers loved coming in and tasting the free samples on offer and this encouraged them to buy much more than they had originally planned. When Carol came home she was very impressed and suggested that we could make our own line of Christmas fare the following year, to include cakes, puddings, chocolate logs and mince pies. We were both very excited at the prospect.

The bombshell hit on the first day of the New Year when I learnt that my David had got engaged to the world renowned soprano, Isabella Rodriguez. There was a photograph of them smiling at each another in the Carmarthen Journal.

I couldn't believe it; I didn't want to believe it. I ripped it up and rushed upstairs, threw myself on my bed and wept and wept until I fell asleep. Carol came over to see me that evening – she had also seen the newspaper that morning. She hugged me and said he was going through a peculiar phase in his life. He'd probably fallen for the glamour and exposure which would benefit his own career.

'She's years older than him,' said Carol.

'But ever so beautiful,' I replied.

'Right, miss you are going to make a New Year's Resolution. You are going to forget about David Meredith and you're going to go out there and find yourself a new boyfriend. Okay?'

'Okay,' I replied without much enthusiasm or conviction.

As it happened I didn't have to go out there looking for anybody – he sort of came to me. It was towards the end of January that we enrolled an extra member to the choir. He was the new history teacher, in what was still the Grammar School, in Carmarthen. He was young and quite good looking in a boyish way and he had a decent baritone voice – it was your father, Alun. We got on well from the outset and he found the story of my career choice interesting. He never told me I should have gone to University to pursue my music – he only told me never to give up playing the piano. We soon started going out together and I found him to be easy company. He would pop into the shop unexpectedly on his way home from work and bring me a book which he thought I'd like to read – they were usually a bit highbrow for me but I took them anyway as I didn't want to hurt his feelings. Mam seemed to like him and so did Aunty Doreen who visited us often. He was invited over for supper one evening. Both my mother and aunt agreed that he was the steady, feet-on the-ground, family type of man. As time passed, I realised that he could be the one for me. Mind you, fireworks didn't erupt when he touched me but it was a gentler, less unpredictable relationship than I had had with David. I thought it would probably be better for me – he was dependable, kind and he was willing to live in the area (as his family came from Swansea) which was a very important factor.

Our romance moved gently along and I was feeling quite contented until one morning, when we were together in Carmarthen, we bumped into David. We just stared at one another and I could feel that magic was still there between us. We were drawn together as always and but for the fact that Alun was standing next to me I'm sure we would have kissed right in the middle of the street. I tried to pull myself together and introduce him to Alun and in a shaky voice I managed to congratulate him on his engagement. He told me he had been awarded a scholarship to study in Milan for a year so he was visiting his parents before he left. I was genuinely pleased for him. Alun invited him to come with us for a coffee but I was relieved when he declined because I don't think I could have stood it. He kissed me on the cheek and secretly squeezed my hand before leaving. I could have done with a stiff drink, rather than the coffee because my legs felt very wobbly. Alun said,

'Come on, you're shivering although it's a really warm day. Perhaps you're sickening for something.'

'I'll be fine when I've got some hot coffee inside me.' It took more than coffee to lift my spirits after that encounter. I think this is a good place to break off.

All my love, always

MamXXX

Although it was well past midnight when Beth eventually came out of the study, she could nevertheless hear Ceri moving about in her room. Beth didn't want to intrude but went up to ask her daughter if she'd like to come down and join her in the kitchen for a mug of cocoa which would, perhaps help her sleep. Ceri seemed pleased that her mother had asked her because she couldn't relax with all her problems racing about in her head. She wanted her mother's opinion on certain matters before she came to a final decision about her future.

'Mam, what would happen if I decided to keep the baby?' asked Ceri.

'What do you mean by what would happen?'

'How would I look after it? Would I be able to work? Would it be fair on the child not to be living with the father?'

Beth took a deep breath before attempting to tackle so many sensitive issues. She firstly tried to instil in her daughter that whatever she decided she would not be alone and would have her, David's and Carol's unwavering support. She then asked Ceri what she was going to do about Matt. Ceri had evidently thought long and hard and had decided that whatever she did about the baby, she did not want Matt O'Connor in her life any more.

'The girls warned me not to get involved with the bastard and I can see now why. Everybody told me that he uses people especially silly, vulnerable women.'

'Don't beat yourself up about it, *cariad* – he was just one of life's mistakes. However, when I was expecting you, I loved David more than life itself and desperately wanted his child. You have to decide whether you want Matt's baby, even though you don't have that love for the father.'

Ceri placed her hands flat on her stomach and said in small voice that she wanted to keep the baby anyway, because she knew that she would love him or her. She told Beth how Matt would go berserk if the story got out that she was expecting his baby. Hardly anybody knew that Ceri was even seeing him, let alone living with him. Her mother told her that it was entirely up to her whether she spilt the beans on him, knowing that if the story got out Ceri could make some money out of it which could come in useful with the baby on its way. Ceri just nodded, thinking that she would wrestle with that problem later on. Beth put on her matter-of-fact voice and announced that certain arrangements would have to be made as early as the following day. Ceri would have to phone her musical director, to tell him exactly what was happening. Hopefully she could continue performing well into her pregnancy. Beth was a little hesitant at bringing up David's offer of accommodation but she decided to throw caution to the wind and mentioned the proposal. Ceri was very quiet for a long time, trying to come to terms with what her mother had just suggested. She realised that in lots of ways it would be the perfect solution but she hadn't yet accepted the fact that David Meredith was her real father. Beth could see she was battling with the situation so advised she left that decision until the following day when she could have a word with David in order that he could explain how things could work. Ceri seemed content with that plan. Ceri then realised how tired she felt so told her mother that she was going up to bed and they could talk again in the morning.

Beth sighed as she watched her only daughter going up the stairs and wondered what the future would be like for her and her child. She then turned back towards the kitchen, smiling to herself at the exciting prospect of becoming a grandmother.

Chapter 12

Beth was surprised to hear Ceri on the telephone shortly after nine thirty the following morning. She busied herself making toast and coffee as she strained to hear what her daughter was saying and to whom. It soon became evident that she had contacted the musical director of Mama Mia. When Ceri came into the kitchen she told her mother that he had been very understanding and that there was no need for her to worry about work. He had suggested that she continue in her present role for a few more weeks and then move back into the chorus until she was ready to leave to have the baby. Beth asked her how she felt about that and Ceri assured her that she couldn't have hoped for more – he had been very fair. Ceri also admitted that her current part was very demanding with two performances most days, so going back to the chorus would give her more time to rest and would be less stressful generally. Just as Beth was pouring the coffee, Carol dropped by on her way to work. She thought that Ceri's news was very exciting and said that she looked forward to babysitting when the time came. Beth reminded her that Ceri would probably be living in London so Carol suggested they both go up as often as possible to spoil the child.

Ceri's next task wasn't so easy – she needed to speak to David but asked Beth if she could talk to him first and explain the situation. David, as Beth suspected, was over the moon regarding Ceri's decision and explained that Ceri was more than welcome to have the large en-suite bedroom at the back of the apartment which was quiet and private. She could lead her own life without his interference but in the knowledge that there was somebody there if she needed anything. Beth conveyed this information to her daughter and then handed her the phone. Fortunately David broke the ice and spoke to Ceri easily, as he had always done, telling her that their relationship didn't have to change but he would feel honoured to be there for her if and when she needed him. So that was sorted – Ceri was to go back to London the following Sunday and start back at work on the Monday. It seemed to Ceri that fate was intervening and forcing her to accept her mother and David's relationship, come what may.

There was one more obligatory call that Ceri needed to make that morning – it was crucial that she talked to *Mamgu,* (Alun's mother).

'What shall I say to her, Mam?'

'Tell her the truth about Matt and the baby but I wouldn't mention the living with David bit. She'll only ask awkward questions and I really don't want her to know the truth – it would hurt her terribly. She's an old woman who's not long lost her youngest son – I wouldn't want to cause her any additional distress. I hope you'll stick with me on that one.'

Mrs. Rees told Ceri to pass the phone to her mother as soon as she'd heard her granddaughter's news, which Ceri was more than willing to do. Elsie Rees thought it was quite disgusting the way young people behaved these days,

'And she's talking about keeping the child? What on earth will people say?'

'Probably not much – it's a new world – unmarried mothers are the norm these days.'

'What are you going to do about the situation Bethan?'

'Nothing really, except give her all my support, as I hope you will.'

Mrs. Rees was not getting the answers she had hoped for so she went on to ask what Matt O'Connor was going to do to help. Beth explained that he didn't want anything to do with the baby so Mrs Rees thought that Ceri should fleece him for every penny she could – take her story to the paper – they'd pay her well. Beth warned her mother-in-law not to mention the situation to anybody as it was up to Ceri what she wanted to do about Matt. When they got rid of Elsie Rees at last, both mother and daughter looked at each other and burst out laughing, mainly from the relief that that most difficult task of the day had been dealt with. Ceri decided that she was going to spend the afternoon shopping in town so it gave Beth the chance to write another of her letters.

Dear Ceri,

I'm so glad that I've decided to write my story because now it will be something for my grandchild as well as you. It's important for us all to know as much of our personal history as possible. At least your child will have a part of his or her genealogy mapped out.

Back to the story: That May Carol became engaged to some chap she'd met in Cardiff. He was studying Psychology at the University. His name was Duncan Randal and was originally from Henley-on-Thames. It had been a whirlwind romance and when she brought him home for the week-end I really didn't take to him. He just didn't fit in to our rural, Welsh community at all – it wasn't his fault – he came from an entirely different background. I felt sorry for Carol's farming parents because I'm sure the situation was difficult for them. He had apparently made a dreadful fuss when he landed in a cow pat as he'd stepped out of his car in his very expensive shoes– he always dressed as if he was going to work in 'the city.' Fortunately he was besotted with Carol, so much so that he was willing to look for work in the area after graduating, to be near her and he bought her a magnificent emerald and diamond engagement ring. She'd told him all about the business and he seemed to be okay about it, so I wasn't too concerned when I heard he was going to pay us a visit. I had to laugh when he came to inspect the shop for the first time. His jaw dropped - I think he expected to see a huge supermarket or something.

'Am I really expected to bury myself in this backwater for this?' He looked close to weeping, poor man. I didn't know what to say in case I made things worse, so I just stood there smiling incongruously. Carol tried to explain all our hopes and plans for the place, wishing that her enthusiasm would rub off on him. At that moment I hoped and prayed that he and Carol would not get married. Unfortunately Alun and Duncan didn't hit it off either, which was a bit awkward. Alun called him a 'conceited, pompous prig' and I tended to agree with him.

Carol and I on the other hand carried on scheming and decided to turn the old store room, where my father had kept potatoes and such things, into a pretty tea room. My Bank Manager was willing to lend us some money to convert it (things like that were much easier then) and Mam gave us her blessing. It was going to be ready by the time Carol completed her College course, that summer.

By that time her big romance with pompous Duncan was over - he had decided that Cwm Rhedyn was definitely not for him as he was more suited to the bright lights of London. Carol did not seem overly upset and I was secretly relieved. He had allowed her to keep the ring, which she said could provide her with some extra cash if ever she needed it. Carol and I worked well together and the business went from strength to strength. I continued with my duties in the choir and my romance with Alun plodded along smoothly. I think it was at the end of November that I heard the news – David and Isabella were to be married the following spring. I also heard on the Cwm Rhedyn grapevine that they were going to be visiting his parents over Christmas. I actually tried to think of somewhere to go over that period just in case I bumped into them but Carol told me I was being ridiculous so I had to hope that I wouldn't see them. It was worse than I expected – he actually brought her to the shop to meet me and Carol. David pulled Isabella towards the counter, where we both stood as if dumbstruck.

'Come and meet my two favourite girls in the whole world, apart from you of course,' he said to his absolutely ravishing fiancé – nobody could argue that she was stunning. 'Beth and Carol are my oldest, dearest friends and they are running this business together.'

I wanted to cry because nobody can change from a lover to a mere friend – you either hate one another or you still have feelings for each other. Isabella thought the shop was magical and she thoroughly enjoyed her afternoon tea prepared by Carol's fair hand. I cannot remember saying much at all – Carol did all the talking. She took Isabella to browse around the shop and show her some of the exciting items we had ordered for Christmas. It was then that David asked if we could make it over to Spain for the wedding. I looked straight at him and said quietly and slowly as if trying to make a child understand something serious and important.

'You will never see me at your wedding – I cannot believe you asked me.' My voice cracked and I could feel hot tears surfacing. 'I wish you well.' David came over and put his arms around me, suddenly realising how much I was hurting.

'I'm so sorry my darling Beth. I thought you wanted to get rid of me – you said so in your letter.'

'I never wanted to let you go but I had no choice. I would kill your ambition and your fantastic career. Isabella can help you and she isn't a stick-in-the-mud who will not leave home.' David stood there looking bewildered. We could hear Carol and Isabella returning from the back storeroom.

'Go to her David,' I whispered. 'Good luck.' They left shortly after that and I burst into tears. Carol said she couldn't believe that David could be so insensitive as to bring that woman to the shop and then if that wasn't enough, he had to ask us to go to his wedding! She announced that men were the most stupid creatures. I didn't tell her exactly what had gone on between us because it felt too private, somehow. Alun called on his way home from school and suggested we went to see a film showing in the Lyric that evening. I must admit that 'Zulu' wasn't going to pull me out of my depressed state so I feigned a migraine. He advised me to go and lie down as I was looking quite pale and I persuaded him to go and see the film as I knew he would enjoy it. After closing the shop and having a quick chat and cup of tea with Carol, I did go up to my room to lie down and try to relax but instead the tears came. Mam must have heard me so she came and sat on the bed, looking down at me shaking her head.

'He always does it to you doesn't he love. David shouldn't have come and he certainly shouldn't have paraded that woman in front of you. You must try and let him go Beth or he'll destroy your life.'

'But I still love him, Mam and he loves me,' I wailed.

'So why are you still here? Why hasn't he taken you with him?'

'Because I told him to go. Because I can't give him the support in his career that Isabella can. Because I'm a timid mouse of a person who hasn't the guts to follow him wherever he goes.' I was shouting now.

'Then Beth you will suffer,' said my mother quite sternly. 'Promise me you won't play about with that nice, young man you're going out with – he deserves better.' She turned and went downstairs, closing the door behind her. My mind was in turmoil because I really wasn't sure if I was doing the right thing. Perhaps I should have followed him – I don't know. My life would have been very different – that I do know.

I wonder what you will think of me for being such a coward.

I'll finish there

All my love

Mam XXX

Chapter 13

Beth and her daughter spent some quality time together for the remainder of Ceri's stay. They went shopping and ate out in a stylish new restaurant in town. They went for walks and took flowers to place on Alun's grave, where Beth became quite emotional,

'Your father would be thrilled about the baby. It's so sad that he won't be here to see him or her.'

'Do you really mean that, Mam?'

'Of course I do. Your father was a good man, Ceri. Don't you ever forget it. Life can be very complicated and stuff just gets in the way sometimes.'

The two women left the cemetery arm in arm, both deep in thought. When they arrived back at the house they found Carol waiting for them as she wanted to say goodbye to Ceri before she returned to London the following day. It was good to have Carol around to lighten the mood. She had been catering for some important corporate do and had brought some delicious food which was left over from the event. So they opened a decent bottle of wine to accompany it. Ceri drank fruit juice and told them she didn't mind because she was now taking the pregnancy seriously and was really looking forward to being a mum. Beth and Carol smiled at each other feeling that perhaps things would turn out alright for them after all.

Ceri was travelling up to London by train and David would be meeting her at Paddington so Beth felt comfortable that her daughter would not be alone. She, on the other hand, felt very lonely, and not for the first time since Alun's death. At least life had been hectic until the funeral with plenty to organise and worry about but suddenly there was nothing and she missed Ceri very much. For some reason she felt an inexplicable jealousy towards David who would now have their daughter all to himself. Beth could not understand these feelings at all. Since Ceri's birth she had hoped that David could be a proper father to their daughter some day but now that it was happening strong memories of Alun kept forcing themselves into the forefront of her mind bringing with them enormous feelings of guilt. She was very unsettled. She didn't want to watch television or read. She was not in the frame of mind to write a letter to Ceri. In the end she decided to go out into the garden and started pulling up the weeds as if her life depended on it. The action gave her a great sense of achievement. She decided that perhaps she should take more interest in the garden and even re-design it to suit her limited capabilities. She smiled to herself and thought how proud Ceri would be of her when she next visited. She just had time to have a bath and scrub her dirty nails before David's daily phone call.

David was there to meet Ceri as promised. He was glad to see her looking better than she had done the previous week. Their meeting was a bit strained at first and Ceri admitted in the car that she felt uncomfortable calling him Uncle David now, as it seemed a bit false, so David suggested she call him just David which seemed to satisfy her. Ceri's room in the apartment was huge and beautifully furnished with its own luxurious en-suite bathroom. He had also put in a kettle, some crockery and cutlery, a small refrigerator and a microwave so that his daughter had as much independence as possible. He also informed her that a lady came in to clean twice a week so she wouldn't have to think of such things. It wasn't that he didn't want Ceri to have the run of the house but thought it was going to take time for them to feel comfortable in each other's company. David suggested they both stuck their weekly work schedules up on the kitchen notice board so they could keep tabs on each other. Ceri thought that was sensible and started to believe that perhaps their living arrangements could actually work. David told her that he was going to phone her mother before making her some tea. Ceri declined explaining that tea made her feel sick and if he didn't mind she would like a short nap as she felt very tired.

Beth was pleased to know that everything seemed to be working out but didn't mention how lonely she felt or the other complex feelings that kept disturbing her but David sensed she wasn't quite herself. He however decided not to pursue the matter for the time being.

Beth felt better as the days passed – choir practices started and she decided to have the garden landscaped with decking, gravel and plants in pots as Ceri had suggested. She continued to buy bits and pieces for the house so that it looked bright and welcoming and of course Carol was always there in the background ready for a chat, a cup of coffee, or a meal. David called her every day with his report on their daughter and Ceri phoned or sent the occasional text message when she had a free minute within her busy schedule.

David made sure that Ceri registered with a good doctor who gave her a date for her first ultrasound scan. She was getting over the sickness faze and David made sure there were plenty of foodie treats available to tempt her. Ceri realised she was being spoilt and was secretly enjoying it. Work was making her so tired that when she had time off, she found herself sleeping for hours. She decided to ask if she could go back to the Chorus as soon as possible as being the leading character was taking too much of a toll on her in her condition. On the day of the scan, Ceri didn't want David to accompany her. He was disappointed but respected her wishes. He did however insist that his chauffeur took her there and back. From the scan they were able to give her a due date and she had a photograph (which looked just like a blob) to take home to show David.

He was so exited that he phoned Beth immediately but felt that she was somewhat cool towards him, which was strange. He asked her if she was alright but even though she said she was fine, David knew that there was something troubling her. On the spur of the moment he told her that he was coming to Cwm Rhedyn the following day for a short break from his hectic schedule. Beth sounded as if she was really pleased. David was determined to get to the root of the problem (whatever it was) and sort it out.

Beth knew she had been distant with David but she couldn't help it. Once he mentioned Ceri's scan and the photograph of the foetus which he had got to see before her, Beth felt the angry jealousy build up in her once again. Later she felt silly and selfish – after all she had had Ceri for all the years, perhaps it was only fair for David to have a little of his daughter now.

That evening David arrived home about half an hour earlier than Ceri. He heard her come in and rush to her room without wishing him goodnight. After a few minutes he tiptoed to her bedroom door and heard her crying. Although David tried his best not to interfere, he had to make sure she was alright. He tentatively knocked on the door and after a few minutes Ceri opened it, her face stained with tears.

'Whatever's the matter? Are you alright? Is the baby alright?'

Ceri asked him if he'd make her a cup of coffee and she would come over to the sitting room and explain what had happened. Apparently she was on her way home and as she rounded the corner at the back of the theatre she was confronted by Matt O'Connor. It had been a bit of a shock. He asked her if she had got rid of the 'brat' and when she told him she had decided to keep the baby he became angry, grabbing her arm roughly and pinning her to the wall. He warned her if anybody tried to drag his name into this fiasco there would be serious trouble. Ceri promised that she was not going to spill the beans and she would try to persuade the few people who knew the truth not to divulge their secret but she did mention that someday when he or she turned eighteen, their child may want to find him and she would be unable to stop that from happening.

'You see Matt, our troubles will always find us in the end. I honestly hope for the child's sake that he or she will never want to find you because you would be a great disappointment.'

'If it's a boy I can guarantee he won't be looking,' replied Matt.

Ceri didn't understand his last statement but she didn't pursue it as she wanted to get home as quickly as possible, so she shrugged him off and hailed a taxi. David couldn't believe that this 'pin-up,' who was adored by his fans, could be such a bastard. He felt that everybody should know what a scum bag he really was but Ceri persuaded him to let it drop as she didn't want anything more to do with Matt. She realised she'd have to talk to the girls with whom she'd shared the house to warn them against leaking any information. She also asked David to make sure that her mother warned Carol and more importantly, *Mamgu*. David was worried that this man could become desperate and do something nasty so when Ceri had gone to bed he telephoned Matt and warned him to keep away from Ceri or the police would be involved. Matt laughed scornfully and said,

'Funnily enough you and I are in the same boat mate. I don't suppose your fans or those people in that Welsh backwater would take it too kindly if they knew that you were Ceri's real dad. So as long as everybody keeps his or her trap shut everything will be fine for both of us.'

With that he put the phone down, leaving David feeling very angry but also realising that what Matt had said was actually true. He'd have to have a long discussion with Beth about all the implications. He was too angry and tired to call her that night and he felt it was something that should be done face to face. He saw Ceri fleetingly the following morning and told her that in future his chauffeur would take her to and from work. She was about to protest but realised how serious David was taking the matter so she accepted his offer graciously. David was also worried about leaving her alone in the apartment whist he was at Cwm Rhedyn but when Ceri pointed out that the place was more secure than Fort Knox, they both laughed and realised that perhaps they were becoming paranoid.

When Beth heard David's car sweeping up the drive, she rushed out to meet him. She held out her hand and dragged him into the house so that she could wrap her arms around his neck and kiss him longingly.

'Wow, Mrs Rees that was worth coming all the way to Cwm Rhedyn for.'

'There's a lot more where that came from.'

'Oh you brazen hussy,' laughed David as they walked arm in arm through to the kitchen where Beth had baked some fresh scones. David looked at her and asked should they have tea first or was there something more important they should be doing.

Smiling Beth replied,

'There's no rush anymore, *cariad*. We don't have to watch the clock – we're free to enjoy one another and the scones!'

David laughed, kissed her quickly and said that the scones did indeed look tempting and he could do with a cup of tea after his drive.

Their need for each other was so strong that they didn't make it upstairs but just went into the sitting room and made love on the rug in front of the fire until they were both sated. They propped a couple of cushions under their heads and pulled the furry throw off the settee to cover them and dozed off in each other's arms for more than an hour.

When Beth awoke she felt very stiff and when she realised what time it was she woke David because she suspected Carol would call on her way from work. They both joked that it was the most exercise they'd had for a long time. They managed to tidy the room and make themselves look presentable before Carol arrived but she guessed what they'd been up to from Beth's flushed face and neck. Carol was so glad for both of them – it had been a long time coming. She wasn't planning to stay long because she appreciated that David and Beth needed time alone but planned to dine with them the following evening. David had made a copy of the scan photograph which he showed them both. He thought Beth would have been anxious to see it but instead she became distant again so he decided to sort whatever was wrong once Carol had left.

'Beth I know you too well so don't think you're kidding me – what is wrong with you? It seems that every time I mention Ceri or the baby you become quiet and distant.'

Beth didn't know what to say but she also knew David too well and recognized he wouldn't drop the matter. She held his hand and looked at him straight in the eyes,

'I feel rather silly, really. I'm jealous of you.' There she had said it.

David looked at her with a puzzled expression.

'What on earth do you mean?'

Beth continued, 'Ceri has always been mine and mine alone. I know Alun was there but I knew she wasn't his. Now you are there to do things for her and be the first to see the scan photo so it suddenly it hit me that she wasn't just mine any more but yours also.'

David couldn't believe what he was hearing but as usual kept very calm. He told her that he could see her dilemma but she had to remember that she, nor anybody else, could own another person, especially Ceri. Their daughter was an independent, grown woman who at best could depend on them both for love and support whatever happened. Beth looked at him and said she was so sorry but she was finding it difficult to cope with her life changing so completely in such a short time. David suggested that perhaps she aught to come up to London more often in order to see Ceri on a regular basis and be there for her next scan. Beth nodded and kissed him for being so understanding.'

David thought it was time to bring up the subject of Matt. He related the whole story and pressed on Beth the importance of people keeping their mouths shut. Beth became worried but David guaranteed that everything would settle down and he'd keep a close eye on Ceri. She decided to contact Alun's mother immediately (not mentioning that David was staying with her of course). David wanted to know what the baby should call him because if he was known as *Tadcu*, the whole story would come out and people would get hurt. Beth thought how complicated everything was becoming and realised it was her own fault for telling Ceri the truth. There was enough time before the birth to address that problem

'By the way, where are we sleeping tonight?' asked David 'I'm not sleeping on my own I hope.'

Beth hadn't really thought about it but decided on the spur of the moment to move to the spare bedroom. She still couldn't have sex with him in the bed she'd shared with Alun. She suggested that they should go into town the following day to choose new wallpaper, carpet and soft furnishings together so as to make it their room. David thought it was a great idea and felt that it was a positive step forward to their future together.

Their day in Carmarthen was fun and they were really pleased with their new purchases which they had chosen together. It surprised them when they both went for the same colours and designs. It proved how well in tune they were with each other. The evening spent with their friend Carol was very enjoyable, as always, and passed far too quickly. As they were preparing for bed, Beth mentioned how much she was going to miss him but she'd make sure the bedroom in its new guise would be ready by the next time he came to visit. To her astonishment he started talking to her about retirement and taking time off to enjoy her, his daughter and the new life ahead of them. Beth was flabbergasted as she could never imagine David not singing any more. He explained that the rigours of his daily routine were taking their toll and he didn't want to carry on singing after his voice was past its best as some opera singers had done. He would hate to be pitied or indeed mocked by the public. Beth wanted to know what he'd do with himself and where would he live.

'I've only just started considering it seriously, so it won't be happening immediately but I think we should keep both the London apartment and this house so that we can go back and forth together or separately. What do you think, Mrs Rees?'

'I'm overwhelmed. I need time to take this in – it's such a big decision for you but if it means I'll be seeing more of you, then bring it on!'

They made love slowly, savouring their every moment together and later slept relaxed in each other's arms.

Chapter 14

David's departure did not leave Beth feeling as downhearted as usual because she had lots of things to look forward to. Before writing one of her letters to Ceri, she contacted the local painter and decorator and arranged for him to wallpaper and paint her and David's bedroom. She then phoned the carpet shop to set up a date for them to come to fit the new carpet. She felt satisfied with herself and made some coffee to take with her to the study where she began to write.

Dear Ceri

I've just heard from David that you're coping and settling in to your new living arrangements. It makes me so glad.

Now back to my saga: David and Isabella got married at the end of May and there were photographs in the national newspapers and the Carmarthen Journal. I could hardly look at them. I tried to study his expression – was he smiling? Did he look happy? Did he look as if he loved her? She was looking adoringly at him and I wanted to drag her away shouting

'Don't you dare touch him, he's mine,' but the truth was that he wasn't mine and never would be. Isabella looked beautiful and very Spanish in lots of lace with a sort of mantilla on her head. Shortly after their wedding, I met Anita, David's sister, in town and we went for a cup of coffee together. She was finishing at Trinity College, Carmarthen (as it was called then) in the summer and had a primary teaching post all lined up for her in a nearby village. I liked Anita but we hadn't mixed a great deal in the past as she was younger than our gang. I chanced to ask her what she thought of Isabella. She replied,

'She's pleasant enough but she's different, not one of us. If she makes David happy, well that's all that matters, isn't it?' Could she make David really happy I wondered. Indeed I was selfish enough to hope she couldn't and he'd come running back to me. I knew I'd thrown away my chance and he'd turned to somebody else. I had to live with it. I kept that newspaper cutting with all the others relating to David's career in a locked box under my bed, which is now up in the attic. After that initial meeting, Anita and I became firm friends and she joined my choir. She also accompanied Carol and me for a meal out sometimes or we went to see girly films together when I knew Alun wouldn't want to come. It was also an opportunity to hear all the news about David and his whereabouts. I bought everything he had ever recorded from vinyl to tapes and later C.D's. The silly thing was that every time I listened to him sing, I cried my eyes out. If for some reason I felt particularly miserable I would listen to him as if I wanted to punish myself. Many's the time you or your Dad would find me listening to the music with tears streaming down my face. How you both teased me about it!

Once I knew David was married I decided I'd have to sort my own life so when Alun asked me to marry him, I accepted and we got engaged on my birthday. I knew Mam was uneasy about it and Carol asked me several times if I thought I was doing the right thing. I know your Mamgu believed your Dad could have done better for himself. Possibly that was true but I didn't think I had any choice. We were to be married the following summer in Ebenezer Chapel with Carol and Anita as bridesmaids and Alun's brother, Tony, as best man. The reception was to be held at The Ivy Bush which as you know is still going strong and Carol and I often meet there for a cup of coffee. Carol offered to make the dresses and the wedding cake – that was be to her really generous gift to us.

It was the day before the wedding and I was in an extreme state of anxiety. The thought of getting married was stressful enough but that morning Anita had telephoned me to say that David was home for the week-end and would call to see me that evening. Mam had gone to Llanelli to visit her sister, Doreen so I knew not to expect her home until about ten o' clock. Alun said he'd pop in for a few minutes, after he'd finished his list of tasks just to check that everything was all set for the following day. I was in a terrible state –I couldn't sit still, I couldn't eat anything and my palms were sticky and wet. When the door bell rang I knew it was David because it was too early for Alun. I tried to calm down and look serene before answering the door.

He stood there with the most beautiful bouquet of red roses – two dozen in all.

'For the bride,' he whispered. I felt tears well up in my eyes and was so choked that I could only nod before closing the door. He grabbed my arm as we walked down the hallway and swung me around until I couldn't avoid looking at him. It just happened again, that infernal chemistry took over. I was in his arms. He kissed my neck, my cheek, my eyes and my mouth. The embrace became more passionate.

'Beth we must get out of here. I want you so much,' he said huskily. I knew I had to stop this – I was getting married to someone else the following day.

'David, my darling we have to stop this, Alun's due here any minute.

'What the hell's going on? You can't get married. You don't love him. You love me.'

'Well you got married – you married Isabella or don't you remember? Doesn't she count any more? David, if we're going to survive we must stop this torture'

As if by magic, Alun saved the day. He rushed in, kissed me on the cheek and asked,

'How's my favourite girl? Are you all set for the big day? He suddenly noticed David and went over to shake his hand. They chatted like old friends and Alun opened a bottle of Champagne to celebrate the moment. As I hadn't eaten anything all day, it went straight to my head. I couldn't believe my ears when I heard Alun asking David to join us at the wedding the following day. Thank God David had the sense to decline but secretly I wondered if the reason he turned down the invitation was that he couldn't bear to witness me marrying another man. Alun said he wasn't staying long and I hoped and prayed that David would also have the sense to leave. It worked out to my advantage when Alun asked David if he could have a lift with him into town as he needed to check some last minute things at the hotel. So both my men left together and I stood shivering on the doorstep even though it was the end of July.

I went up to bed about ten and heard Mam arrive home shortly afterwards. I couldn't sleep much that night and my mother found me drinking tea at the kitchen table around three in the morning.

'Couldn't you sleep love? Most people suffer from pre-wedding nerves you know. I think I'll have a cuppa with you,' she said pulling up her chair next to mine. 'Hey, did Alun buy you those beautiful roses; they must have cost him a fortune?'

'No, David did,'

'David? What do you mean?'

'He called last night. He's home for a few days and his mother must have told him I was getting married tomorrow, so he brought me the flowers to wish me well.'

'Oh. I see,' but she didn't sound at all convinced. 'Was Alun here when he called?'

'For part of the time. They got on really well and Alun asked him to come to the wedding but he isn't coming.'

Mam didn't say a word but stirred her tea for a long time wearing a worried look. I felt very uncomfortable.

'Mam, what's bothering you?'

'I'm not sure, Beth. I always feel uneasy when David's about. The attraction between you two has always been so strong that sometimes I think he has some sort of hold over you.'

'Don't be silly, Mam. David's married and I never see him these days. He's singing all over the world for goodness sake. Surely we can still be friends? Remember I'm getting married in the morning.'

'Yes, yes of course. I'm sorry love,' she said but she did not sound fully assured. I made my way towards the door,

'I'd better try and get some beauty sleep. See you in the tomorrow, Mam.' I kissed her cheek and left her sitting in the kitchen. I wondered what was going through her mind. It concerned me.

Next morning I didn't have time to think of anything other than getting ready for my big day. The wedding gown Carol had made for me was lovely. It was a flattering ankle length, Empire style dress in a rich cream crepe material with a guipure lace bodice. My dark hair had been swept up high with ringlets falling down the back and whispy curls framing my face.(Of course you've seen the photographs)I felt like a Jane Austen heroine but I knew I wasn't going to marry my Mr Darcy. As I walked out of the door on my Uncle Harry's arm, I swapped my wedding bouquet for the red roses, David had given me. It was a silly thing to do and although I'm certain Mam realised what I had done, she never mentioned it.

It was a lovely wedding and the sun shone for the photographs. The reception meal was first class, although Alun's mother complained that hers was cold, and the speeches were too long. I went to change after the food as we were driving up to the Lake District for our Honeymoon,. (We didn't have evening parties in those days.) Mam squeezed my hand and wished me good luck as I got in the car. I think she knew I would need it.

Well Ceri, love, I feel a little drained after this chapter so I'll finish for now.

Love Mam xx

David had been back in his apartment for less than an hour when the telephone rang. He'd only had time to contact Beth, make himself a cup of coffee and unpack his overnight case. He was extremely surprised to hear Matt O'Conner's voice.

'What do you want?' asked David gruffly.

'Listen I don't want to make trouble but I do want to see you so that I can explain a few things. I'd like to do this as soon as it's feasible. It's very important.'

'Do you want Ceri to be present?' questioned David.

'Not initially. I'd like a word with you on your own first if that's possible.'

David considered for a moment before deciding to invite him over for coffee the next morning. He knew Ceri had her weekly dance class and would be going straight from there to the theatre. He was intrigued and puzzled as to what Matt wanted. It was pointless letting Beth know about the meeting; he would contact her as soon as he discovered what it was all about. Ceri came home at her usual time that night and seemed pleased to see that he had returned. She looked tired but ensured him that she had been fine on her own and wanted to know if her mother was coping. David was able to set her mind at rest.

Matt arrived at half past ten, the following morning. David was glad to see that he was not in an aggressive mood so invited him in. They sat in the sitting room facing one another.

'Well,' said David, 'I was rather surprised to hear from you so what's it all about?'

Matt apologised for his behaviour the last time they had spoken but hoped that David would forgive him after hearing what he had to say. David could see that Matt was finding whatever it was very difficult so he let him take his time. In the end Matt explained that there was a medical condition, called Tay Sach's Disease, which was a genetic disorder and he was a carrier of the disease. People from Jewish descent, as he was, were more prone to the condition. His real name was Michael Garten and his parents had immigrated to Ireland shortly after the war. He did not suffer from the disease himself but was able to carry it to his children in various ways. He explained that it was a fatal genetic disorder occurring in children and was caused by the absence of a vital enzyme. David listened sympathetically as Matt told of him that he had lost a three year old son, Thomas, to the disease. A child could only develop the full disease if both parents were carriers and unfortunately his first wife, who was also Jewish, carried the bogus gene. He went on to explain that Ceri's baby would not develop the actual disorder, because it was unlikely that Ceri was a carrier, but the child had a fifty, fifty chance of being a carrier thus enabling the condition to go on and on. He explained that his second wife was not a carrier herself but two of their three daughters, were. Matt explained that he had told Ceri very firmly that he did not want any more children but had not given her any explanations – it retrospect he felt he should have. When Ceri came out with the news that she was pregnant, his whole nightmare started again and he admitted that he had lost it –throwing things across the room in his rage. He never thought that Ceri would want to keep the child as her career had just taken off, so he hadn't bothered to tell her the truth. Now he realised she would have to know everything as she had decisions to make. David sat there for a minute before saying anything.

'Well Matt, I think we could both do with something stronger than coffee.' He went over to the drinks cabinet and brought them both a brandy before asking,

'Does everybody who is born with it die young?'

'Yes usually before the age of five'

'Why did you not develop it?'

'Only one of my parents must have been a carrier so in a way I was lucky. We're not sure where it came from initially. My daughters know the score so the problem carries on. You can read all about it on the internet. Perhaps that would be a good idea before telling Ceri.' David agreed and told Matt that he would persuade Ceri's mother to come up to London before their daughter was told. Matt departed, promised to keep in touch and stressed that he was willing to be present when they told Ceri, in case she had any questions. After Matt's departure, David sat with his head in his hands thinking of his little girl and considering everything she had been through recently. He hoped that this wasn't going to be the last straw.

David had to be in Covent Garden by three o'clock so he decided not to phone Beth until he finished his evening performance. He would have had some time by then to think what he was going to say to her. He lacked concentration that afternoon which was very unlike him, resulting in one or two of the cast asking if he was feeling ill. He ate a light meal before the evening performance and tried to have some quiet time in his dressing room so that he could give of his best. He thought his performance lacked certain lustre but the audience didn't seem to notice because they gave him his usual standing ovation.

Ceri was at home when he returned so he went into his bedroom to telephone Beth. He decided that he would have to tell her the truth – there was no point in kidding her. She was very upset, as he had envisaged, but fortunately Carol happened to be with here so he felt a little more comfortable. David thanked God for Carol once again – she was always there, always so dependable and such a good friend to them both. Beth agreed to come up to London the following day as the decorators weren't due to start until the following week. He went over to tell Ceri. She wanted to know why her mother was coming so unexpectedly but David managed to convince her that Beth was taking advantage of the few days before everything kicked off in the house.

Beth put on a brave face when she met Ceri and the two women spent some time catching up on news. Ceri then left to meet some friends so it gave David and Beth an opportunity to research the disease on the internet. What they read was grim but of course they did realise that Ceri's baby would not inherit the full blown disease. On the other hand there was a certain responsibility to halt the disease by not producing carriers. It became clear that Ceri could opt for an amniocentesis at about sixteen weeks to see if the foetus was carrying the bogus gene. They went out for a meal to try to come to terms with this new problem but were glad to arrive back at the apartment. They contacted Matt and arranged a meeting with him the following day as David knew Ceri had a day off from work. Beth asked her daughter if she had any plans for the following morning. Fortunately she didn't, so her mother suggested they spend the morning with David, as he would be working in the afternoon, and then they could possibly hit the shops. Ceri seemed quite happy with those arrangements.

They had just finished breakfast the following morning when the door bell rang. Ceri was very shocked to see Matt and was about to go to her room when David stopped her. She demanded to know what was going on when her mother told her to sit down and listen to what Matt had to say. Matt relayed the story as he had to David previously. Ceri listened but then turned round and said,

'But that's okay then, my child will not have this Tay Sach's thing.'

'No,' said Matt but the baby would have a strong possibility of being a carrier. This would mean that the disease could go on and on and from time to time two carriers could come together and produce a baby boy who would die in his early years. Ceri started to realise that she had certain responsibilities and started to cry. Matt told her he was very sorry but perhaps she could now at least understand his initial reaction when she had told him the news. Ceri nodded. Her mother told her that she could have the test but she would need to go to see her doctor as soon as possible. Before Matt left he told Ceri that he would answer any questions that she would later think of and was willing to see the doctor with her if it was any help. After Matt had gone, Ceri shut herself in her room and her parents respected her privacy. She stayed there until the evening. David went off to Covent Garden, leaving Beth on her own. She decided to spend the time writing one of her letters mainly because she thought it might help her to deal with this recent ordeal.

Chapter 15

Beth curled up in the corner of the vast settee with her notebook ready to write her next letter, thinking that it would be good for her to try and focus on anything other than Matt's revelation.

My dear Ceri,

It's strange writing to you in David's apartment with you in your room just down the corridor but it gives me something definite and positive to do at this stressful time.

Before going on to describe my married life I feel I must explain the relationship between your mamgu and me because you've always been aware that there are tensions between us. However hard I've tried to hide the fact, I took an instant dislike to your father's mother from the moment I set eyes on her. She was a cold, devious, self-opinionated, outspoken woman and I couldn't believe she had given birth to Alun who was her complete opposite. I can only believe that he resembled his father, whom I had never met. As you know her name is Elsie but it was made clear from the outset that I should call her Mrs Rees, which has continued to this day. I could never have called her Mam or anything endearing as I grew to dislike her more and more over the years. She always called me Bethan, not it's shortened version of Beth - although she knew I hated my full name. Her first words to me when Alun introduced us were,

'Oh! Where on earth did you meet this one, she isn't your usual type?' It made me smile because it gave the impression that your father had a harem whereas he was actually very shy with women. I instantly christened Elsie Rees, The Red Dragon, partly because of her fading red hair and also because she threw flames at me whenever she spoke.

That first meeting formed a pattern which continued throughout our marriage; she would be rude to me, Alun would apologise on her behalf, always finding excuses for her behaviour and I would seethe inside but not utter a word. The relationship with your Mamgu did not help our relationship. I couldn't understand how your father was so tolerant of her especially as she was always singing the praises of his brother, Tony - how well he had done to become a consultant in the Heath Hospital, Cardiff, what a lovely, supportive wife he had and how clever their children were. The whole family made me feel inferior, which was not a great basis for a marriage. It was because your father was not my number one love that I put up with everything. I thought I should be punished for not loving him enough. Throughout everything however, I had a gentle, doting, easy-going husband who adored you. Your Mamgu, I must admit truly loved you (and still does) and you could do no wrong in her eyes so I tried not to antagonise her too much. I remember after one visit, I had been particularly quiet in the car on the way home; your father must have sensed my mood and said,

'Beth, my mother isn't as bad as she seems. She's had a tough time bringing up Tony and myself on her own. My father left us when we were very young (personally I could see why, but I didn't comment.) She only wants what's best for us - she often embarrasses me but I know she means well. When you get to know her better, you'll see she isn't that bad.' I tried to smile but to be honest I was never convinced.

We lived in a small flat above the Butcher's Shop for the first few months after the wedding. It was large enough for just the two of us and it was convenient for your father's school and my shop. It wasn't long before Alun started talking about buying a house and when he saw Tŷ Cerrig he fell instantly in love with the place. I have a feeling that his mother had planted grandiose ideas into his head by always referring to his brother's fabulous home in Cyncoed, Cardiff. I wasn't too keen on the house and I knew it would be a struggle for us to afford such a place but as usual I gave in because I felt that Alun deserved it for marrying me. We moved into our over- large house in the spring when the crocuses carpeted the front lawn – it was very pretty but I never felt much love for the house. Perhaps you've realised that I have had to change certain things in it recently because I needed to feel it was my home and that I wasn't just a visitor. It amuses me to realise that I'm beginning to feel a little affection for the place for the first time in all these years.

Our marriage plodded on quite nicely. Carol had got engaged to Glyn, our local young policeman and Anita flitted merrily from one boyfriend to another. The business was going well and Carol and I were talking seriously about expansion. Life went on without many intense highs or debilitating lows – everything was just middling. I should have been more content. I had a beautiful house, a caring husband, a job I enjoyed, but there was always something missing. Of course I knew what that something was. I read about David in the papers occasionally and I bought all his recordings. He hadn't been back to our neck of the woods since my wedding, for whatever reason. Anita kept me up to speed with his movements and whereabouts but I was careful not to show too much interest. It was about two years into our marriage when she told me that David and Isabella were coming for a week's break to Carmarthen and would be staying at the family home. I panicked and felt I wanted to disappear somewhere in case I met them but I knew that was impossible as it was term time so your father couldn't get away from school. The dreaded week arrived and up until the Wednesday I hadn't seen or heard anything of them. However, that evening Alun came home and announced,

'Guess who I saw in town, lunchtime.' He didn't have to tell me, I had already guessed. He went on to say,

'I've invited them over for a meal on Friday night. Thought it was a nice thing to do. I've asked Carol and Glyn and you could ask Anita and the new bloke she's seeing to join us. We could make an evening of it.' I couldn't believe what he had done. I didn't make a fuss because that would have made him suspicious so I just screamed inside. I couldn't wait to see Carol in the shop the following morning. She understood my problem but couldn't see a way out of it. She told me that I'd just have to cope. We got in touch with Anita who was thrilled to accept the invitation so everything was arranged. Carol was to prepare the meal and I got out all the finery we'd received as wedding gifts. Out came the damask tablecloth and napkins, the Royal Doulton dinner service, the Waterford crystal and the king's pattern cutlery. Alun supplied flowers for the table from his beautiful garden and I attempted to form water lilies out of the napkins, into which we placed bread rolls. I can remember exactly what was on the menu – Melon balls and grapes in sweet white wine, Duck a l'Orange with Duchesse potatoes, followed by a pear and sherry gateau and freshly made coffee from my trusted Russell Hobbs percolator. Alun played the charming host and plied everyone with a different wine for every course, Glyn was pleasant and amusing and Isabella was just simply stunning. I was aware that Carol was studying me because I knew she had noticed that David was very quiet, ignoring his wife most of the time and gazing at me all the time. It made me feel wonderful but very uncomfortable. However, the evening went without a hitch until David suggested he came to the kitchen to help me with the coffee. He came behind me, placing his arms around my waist and nuzzling the back of my neck – I felt myself melt into him. Neither of us uttered a word – there was no need. Goodness knows what would have happened if Carol hadn't come in. She gasped and we jumped apart. She turned and took the petites fours with her. I looked at David and just shook my head as in defeat and took a deep breath before taking out the coffee and acting as if I was having a terrific time. David and Isabella left with Anita and her current boyfriend at about eleven, leaving just your father, myself and Carol and Glyn. Your Dad and Glyn went into the study for a brandy and a cigarette (they were both still smoking then) and Carol and I were left to clean up. Carol looked at me in disbelief,

'What the hell was that all about? You're both married for God's sake.'

I realised then that I had to come clean about the whole complex situation. Carol didn't judge us but warned me that I was wasting my life pining for my impossible love and wouldn't it be better to try and forget David and settle for what I had. Of course she was making a lot of sense but the only thing I could promise was that I'd try to avoid meeting him or contacting him in any way. Apparently Carol met David on his own, the following day and told him that she understood our situation and that it was a pity it couldn't have been different but he had to leave me alone if we and our marriages were to survive. I don't know what else was said.

The next I heard about David was that he was playing Figaro in Rossini's Barber of Seville in La Scala, Milan. Life developed a pattern here in Cwm Rhedyn, we had our work, Alun joined the Golf Club with Glyn. I had my choir and Carol was developing an outside catering branch to our original business. Your father and I travelled around Europe each summer, sleeping in a tent. We loved travelling and as you know we later bought the caravan which offered a bit more luxury. Carol and Glyn got married in the local registry office with me and your father, Glyn's brother and Anita as witnesses. Carol wanted a quiet affair with no fuss and that's exactly what she got. They moved into that huge house on the hill called 'The Gables,' and they seemed very happy at first. Alun and I started trying for a baby but nothing seemed to be happening. My mother told me to seek advice but I didn't want to become obsessed about getting pregnant. We had a decent life and I felt that if it was to be it would happen; it didn't. The more time went on the less often we tried to do anything about it and our sex life waned. It didn't really worry me as that took the pressure off the baby business but it did make me yearn for David even more. One evening in choir practice, Anita told me that her brother was going to be on the radio programme, Desert Island Discs which was to be transmitted later in the spring. I actually tuned in to it regularly so was able to find out the exact date. It would have been better if I hadn't listened to it but then I never did the most sensible things. Amongst his choice of eight discs he naturally included one of his wife, Isabella, singing Un Bel di Vedremo from Puccini's Madam Butterfly, he included a Welsh folk song and a Beatle's song but then he said he had chosen one particular song as it reminded him of a very special friend and his youth – it was our song, Roy Orbison singing 'Golden Days'and I sat there crying my eyes out. He then had to choose a luxury to take with him to the imaginary Island and he said he would take a small painting which he had of his home area, which he took with him wherever he went, around the world. I knew it was the painting of Cwm Rhedyn I had bought for him the first Christmas we were together. At the end of the programme, I felt disturbed and very angry with him. He probably guessed I would be listening and he knew I would understand the inferences. Didn't he realise the effect it would have on me? Thank goodness your father was playing golf so I had time to pull myself together before his return. Anita called that afternoon to see if I'd heard David and she commented on the special friend he had mentioned, wondering who that could have been but I ignored the bait. It took me days to get back on even keel and Carol chastised me for listening to the programme and I think she was annoyed with David for messing with my head.

Your father was made Head of the History department in his school and Carol and I had extended the kitchen at the back of the shop in order to provide a space for all the outside catering work which was coming our way. It was a very exciting and profitable time for the business. People were entertaining in their own homes. The dinner party was getting more and more popular and the women who couldn't cook or went out to work depended on us supplying the food. We were now employing five people and thinking about renting an additional space nearby. The premises were still owned by my mother and she continued to live in the house in the back. She and Gwilym Williams enjoyed each other's company but they didn't get married or anything - perhaps it suited them both that way. One thing that worried me during that period was that Carol and Glyn had relationship problems. Glyn had an affair with a girl from Swansea blaming it on the fact that he hardly saw Carol as she was always working. They managed to patch up the relationship for a while and Carol became pregnant. Everything seemed to be working out but then she had a miscarriage and Glyn had another affair. Things went from bad to worse, ending in their separating and later they divorced and sold the large house on the hill. Carol moved into a newly built much smaller house and she's stayed there ever since. Eventually Anita found a boy she wanted to marry. He taught with her and was extremely handsome. His name was James and they were to have a big splash of a wedding much to the delight of her parents who thought it would never happen. This was eight years after your father and I got married. Carol and Alun and I were invited of course but your father had promised to take some school children on a field trip that week-end so he couldn't come. I knew for certain that David would be present at his only sister's wedding which made me both very excited and scared. I even convinced myself that seeing him there with Isabella and his family would make me realise that time had passed and our relationship had dwindled. Of course fate played its joker - Isabella couldn't be present because she was in The Met, New York and couldn't get out of a prior engagement.

When I showed Mam the invitation and told her that Alun couldn't come, she became quiet before commenting,

'He'll be there, I suppose?'

'Who do you mean?' I said feigning ignorance

'You know very well who I mean – David Meredith.'

'Of course he'll be at his sister's wedding – what's your problem, Mam?'

'I've no problem but don't rock the boat my girl.'

I laughed, gave her a hug and left.

That's it for now Ceri my love,

Mamxxx

Beth was sipping a cup of tea when Ceri entered the room looking bleary eyed.

'Did you have a nap, *cariad*?' enquired Beth, afraid to touch on the subject that occupied both their minds. Ceri explained that she had thought and thought about Matt's revelation and had become so exhausted that she had dropped off to sleep. Beth asked her if she had come to any conclusions.

'Yes, I've decided to ask for an amniocentesis and if the rogue gene is present in the baby, I'm going to have an abortion because it's not fair to carry this horrible disease down through generations.' Beth hugged her daughter, telling her how proud she was of her. When David was told of the decision he also felt extremely pleased that his daughter could be so brave. The following day they made an appointment to see the doctor and he in turn reserved a slot in the hospital's schedule for the test, which could be done when she was fourteen weeks pregnant. She had a few weeks to wait but accepted the situation now that she had made her decision. Beth accompanied her to the hospital and they were told the test results would be available later that week. The amniocenteses showed that the unwanted gene was present in Ceri's baby.

Chapter 16

Both Beth and David were becoming increasingly worried about their daughter. Since the result of the amniocentesis she wasn't communicating with them at all. She existed like an automaton – eating, sleeping and working as was necessary. Beth realised that she had to get back to Cwm Rhedyn as she'd already put off the painters and decorators for a week so decided to confront Ceri that very day in order that they could try to make sense of things. David decided to keep out of the way initially as he didn't want to overdo the concerned father act. Ceri protested that she wasn't ready to talk about things but Beth explained that she would be returning home soon and time was speeding along and if Ceri decided to terminate the pregnancy it would have to be done sooner rather than later. Beth told her daughter that she understood what a difficult position she was in but Ceri started to cry and shout that nobody understood her dilemma, least of all her mother. She wailed,

'In a way I'd be killing a healthy baby because we know that my baby wouldn't contract the disease but on the other hand I could be killing an innocent child down the line as my son or daughter would probably be a carrier. What the hell should I do Mam?'

Her mother didn't have any answers but put her arms around her daughter and held her until the sobbing subsided. Beth suddenly had an idea. She decided to telephone Matt and ask him to come round to speak to Ceri as he was the only one who could answer her questions in order to put things in perspective. He was more than willing to do so and arrived within the hour. Beth made them all some coffee and retreated into the bedroom so that the couple could talk in private. After about an hour there was a knock on her door and Ceri announced that Matt was about to leave. He'd been a great help as he had been able to explain the devastating problems suffered by his little boy. Matt also described the trauma of losing him and the effect it had on their relationship as husband and wife. He didn't think his ex-wife had ever got over it. Ceri wept silently as she listened to Matt recalling the heartbreaking events and realised she couldn't put people through that sort of tragedy even if it was way down the line. In the light of Matt's story she decided to have the abortion and Beth breathed a sigh of relief. When David came home, he was told of the decision and he offered to pay for her to have it done in a private clinic. Beth would come back up to London to be with her. So the following morning they made all the arrangements. Beth went home to Cwm Rhedyn to deal with the decorators before returning to London almost immediately.

Directly after the termination, Ceri seemed positive and returned to work without delay. She had remained in the role of Sophie as the pregnancy hadn't advanced far enough for her to move back into the chorus. Beth was secretly disappointed that she wasn't going to be a grandmother but tried to look at things philosophically, realising that it would be better if Ceri was firstly in a stable relationship before any children came along. She was a little afraid that Ceri would get back with Matt but when she confronted her daughter, Ceri insisted that the affair was over but they remained on friendly terms. David wanted Beth to stay in London for a while but she was itching to get back home to see how the work on their bedroom was progressing. Departures were no longer distressing for either of them because they both knew they could now be together as often as they wished so it became a natural development in their relationship. It also gave them both a few days of private space now and again which was good, as they had never spent long periods together in the past – it was always on borrowed time – so they were eased gently into living together.

Beth was thrilled with the bedroom thus far and was ready to arrange for the carpet to be laid. Her excitement was transmitted to David when she phoned him and he replied that he couldn't wait to see it and try it out! Carol felt so sorry for Ceri when she was told the whole story and she had some sympathy for Matt but thought he should have been honest from the start. Beth decided to tell Alun's mother that Ceri had suffered a miscarriage. Elsie Rees had to add,

'Lucky for you I hadn't told anybody then. Pity I hadn't gone to the papers though – I could have made myself some tidy money. Perhaps I still will.'

'Nobody would believe you as there's no a baby any longer and Ceri and Matt aren't together any more, either', Beth commented and reluctantly invited her over when Ceri was next at home.

A few days passed uneventfully but then Beth had a disturbing call from David. He was worried about Ceri. Her musical director had informed him that Ceri was very miserable and didn't seem to have her heart in her work. David noticed she wasn't eating much and had become pale and irritable and he heard her crying in her bedroom late at night. He told Beth that he was going to persuade Ceri to see the doctor and take some time off because he had a feeling that she would be facing dismissal from work if nothing was done about the matter soon.

Beth decided to return to London the following day and she, with David's help, persuaded Ceri to see her doctor. The doctor thought it would be a good idea if she saw a counsellor who specialised in dealing with post abortion stress. Before the appointment was made, Beth suggested that Ceri came home with her to Tŷ Cerrig for a complete break so arrangements were made to see a counsellor back home in Wales. This wasn't a problem so the women were able to travel back to Cwm Rhedyn the following day and David promised to join them as soon as his work schedule allowed. Beth felt better knowing she could keep an eye on her daughter. It was evident that the abortion had affected Ceri more than anyone had realised. Ceri had her first appointment with the counsellor the following week. Fortunately she liked and trusted the woman and after a few sessions Beth felt there was a marked improvement in her daughter's condition. Carol came to see them often and tried to talk to Ceri about her own feelings after she had miscarried although they weren't quite the same, as Ceri so readily pointed out. Ceri continued to feel very guilty about deciding to abort a healthy baby even though she had done it for all the right reasons. Her mother and Carol hoped the counsellor could get through to her but they both realised it was not going to be a quick return to the old Ceri.

Alun's mother insisted on coming over to see her granddaughter a couple of weeks later. She'd travelled on the train, so Beth felt obliged to ask her to stay the night. Elsie Rees took one look at the pale, miserable girl and without any empathy told Ceri to pull herself together and forget about having babies until she'd found herself a decent man to look after her. Beth could have happily strangled her mother-in-law. Carol didn't venture near when Mrs Rees was in residence and Beth had warned David not to contact her. Naturally Alun's mother wanted to visit her son's grave, so she persuaded Ceri to accompany her. On the way she asked her granddaughter lots of probing questions – how often did she see David Meredith, where was she living now, did she see anything of Matt? Ceri was very careful how she answered the questions because one slip could open a huge can of worms. After all, her grandmother was an old woman and gargantuan shocks, of the type that Ceri could have revealed, could really upset her and break up their relationship completely. Elsie Rees decided to stay another night much to Beth's frustration as the carpet fitters were due and she didn't want her mother-in-law to start asking questions about the room she was decking out for herself and David. Fortunately the carpet fitter hadn't arrived before Beth drove Mrs Rees to Carmarthen to catch the train back home to Swansea. Before she left she wanted to know how long Ceri was staying. Beth stepped in, saying that Ceri had had a tough time of it lately and needed a really good rest. She promised she'd bring her daughter over to see her in the next week or so.

As soon as Mamgu had left, Beth and Ceri felt like some fresh air so they went for a long walk along the river bank in the warm autumn sunshine. On the way home Beth persuaded Ceri to join her for some tea and cakes in the new little teashop as her daughter seemed more relaxed of late. In the Cafe they happened to meet Ceri's best friend, Donna, from her schooldays. She and her two little boys were visiting Donna's parents for ten days because her only brother was coming home for a long awaited holiday from Sydney, Australia where he was working as a corporate lawyer. Neither Donna nor her parents had seen him for over two years and were really excited about the visit. Ceri hadn't seen her school friend for over a year as they never seemed to be in Cwm Rhedyn at the same time. Beth loved seeing the two girls together again; chatting about school days and the silly things they used to do when they were younger. It seemed like only yesterday when Donna and Ceri used to shut themselves in Ceri's bedroom playing their loud music, laughing and eating her out of house and home. The reunion looked as if it was doing Ceri some good so Beth invited Donna over to Tŷ Cerrig the following morning for coffee. Donna said she'd try to escape on her own as she was sure her mother would look after the boys for a couple of hours. Ceri appeared happier on their walk home and her mother thanked her lucky stars they had met Donna. She related the story to David on the telephone that evening and he thought that this could be a breakthrough. Perhaps the company of an old, trusted friend whom Ceri had known all her life would enable her to open up just as Beth herself had done to Carol all those years ago.

Ceri and Donna spent the following morning reminiscing and finding out about one another's present lives. In the end Ceri found herself telling Donna how much she missed her father and the story about Matt, herself and the baby. She also told her friend about David and swore her to secrecy as everybody continued to think he was only her mother's friend and her own godfather. Whilst Donna listened intently she held her Ceri's hand and said,

'What you need now is a complete change of scene. Work can wait and even if you lose this part, there will be others because they know how good you are. Listen, we're having a party in Mum and Dad's house when Steffan arrives home – you've got to come. There will be plenty of people you know there and anyway I'd like you to be around. It's so lovely to see you again. I hadn't realised how much I've missed you and Ceri, remember, I shan't utter a word to anybody about what you've told me about Matt or David Meredith'

Ceri thought for a while about the party invitation as she wasn't sure if she was ready to meet lots of people but Donna was very persuasive and insisted that it would do her some good, so in the end she agreed to go. Donna hugged her and commented as she left,

'It's a great excuse to buy a new dress – we can go shopping together.'

Beth was really pleased with the effect Donna was having on her daughter and the forthcoming party was something positive for Ceri to look forward to. David managed to pay them a visit over the following week-end and was amazed at the change in Ceri. He was also thrilled with the new bedroom and loved sharing it with Beth without feelings of guilt.

Donna and Ceri went to Swansea for some serious clothes shopping. Ceri told her mother that she hadn't enjoyed herself so much in ages. Beth was overjoyed to hear it.

David had to get back to London but left feeling much happier about his daughter's state of mind. He wanted to know if Beth knew when Ceri was likely to return to the city but she said that nothing had been decided and she wasn't pushing it. Secretly David was missing having someone in the apartment. When he left, Beth busied herself doing silly chores that weren't important but it was her way of coping with the separation from David. That night she moved back to the bedroom she had shared with Alun. She had no idea why but felt it was the right thing to do. It was strange that she had waited all the years to be with David but in actual fact it was difficult to break the ties of a thirty year marriage. She felt that it was something she'd have to sort out gradually. After all there was no rush.

Donna contacted Ceri three days before the party to say her brother had arrived and invited her friend to lunch the following day to meet Steffan, adding that her parents would also love to see her again after all this time. Ceri already knew Steffan of course but as he was five years older than Donna and herself they hadn't done much together as children. In actual fact Steffan used to try and escape from the girls whenever he could as they were a nuisance, always trying to follow him and his friends everywhere. Ceri hadn't seen him for years as he'd gone away to university and then worked in London before going over to Australia. It was lovely to meet Donna's parents again and she was told that Steffan would be joining them for lunch. Mrs Pritchard had just called the girls to the table and managed to wash her grandsons' hands when Steffan arrived. He took one look at Ceri and said,

'Wow, the duckling has changed into a swan.' He kissed her on her cheek and they all sat down to a very convivial meal. Ceri tried not to stare at Steffan too much but he was incredibly handsome – his tanned skin and sun-bleached blond hair portrayed the hunky, outdoor look of a stereotype Australian rather than a Welsh boy from Carmarthenshire. Conversation was easy as they all knew each other well and were interested to learn about each other's present lives. Steffan was very impressed with Ceri's star role in the musical and said he'd have to have her autograph. After lunch Steffan took Donna's two boys out to play football in the garden whilst Donna and Ceri cleared the table and stacked the dishwasher.

'What do you think of him then?' asked Donna.

'What are you getting at?'

'Oh come on Ceri I think Steff fancies you.'

'Shut up,' answered Ceri throwing a tea towel at her friend. They both laughed.

Beth came to pick up Ceri in the car at three thirty and asked her how her day had been. Ceri smiled and said,

'Interesting. Let's say I'm quite looking forward to that party on Saturday.'

Beth wondered what her daughter meant by her remark but just by looking at Ceri Beth knew something good had happened.

Chapter 17

When Ceri came downstairs on the night of the party, Beth had to dry a tear from her eye as she recognized how beautiful her daughter had become and so like David. She was also amazed as to how much Ceri's health had improved in such a short time. Ceri looked absolutely stunning and Beth thought it was a pity her father couldn't see her now. For a split second Beth wondered which father she was referring to so decided that they would both be very proud of their only daughter. Beth drove her to Donna's parent's house which was a few miles away. Ceri would be staying with her friend overnight as they had already erected a camp bed for her. This was the opportunity Beth had been waiting for – some time on her own to write one of her letters. It had been a long time since she had written anything at all.

She closed herself in the study and tried to concentrate on what she was going to write next.

Ceri my love,

I'm now coming to the most important part of my story as far as you're concerned.

I bought a long, cotton, Victorian style dress for Anita's wedding – maxis were all the rage. It made me look rather demure with its high neck, pin-tucked bodice and frilled hem. It was made from a pretty, stripy, floral material in subtle shades of mauve and turquoise, which were the 'in colours' of that time. Actually the dress suited my dark colouring and the clipped waistline accentuated my then, slim figure. I didn't wear a hat but pulled the top part of my hair back and tied it with ribbons the same colour as my dress. It made me feel young and frivolous although I was thirty-four by then. Alun thought I looked great and was sorry he couldn't accompany me but it wasn't him that I was trying to impress. Carol was picking me up at the shop that Saturday morning, where Mam came to see us off.

'Enjoy yourselves,' she said and then hesitated as if she was about to say something else but decided against it.

'We will,' I called back 'see you tomorrow with all the news. Remember, Carol and I have booked a room at the hotel for tonight.'

'Bye cariad, be careful.'

I wasn't sure what she meant by those last words or else I didn't want to understand. It was a glorious, sunny June day – ideal for a wedding. The perfume from the roses in Mam's garden made me feel quite heady. At least I blamed my euphoric mood on the sunshine and roses.

The official photographer had set himself up near the main door of the church so that he could take photographs of the guests as they arrived. I was so intent on not tripping in front of the camera that I wasn't aware of anybody coming up behind me until I felt a gentle tap on my arm. There was no need to ask who was there because I knew instinctively it was David. My heart was pounding and I was definitely panicking. I had hoped my emotions were under control because I had practised what I was going to say to him. I had intended to appear calm and sophisticated but in reality his touch had been like an electric shock and I found myself floundering. He bent down and whispered close to my ear,

'God Beth you look beautiful. I'm so glad we're both here.'

I felt like crying because I knew that when I turned around I'd be facing his wife, Isabella. However he spun me around and we looked into each others eyes. We both knew that nothing had changed between us – the old chemistry was still there. For a split second I hadn't even noticed he was alone. He explained that Isabella had other commitments and I told him that Alun also had to go away with the school. We both smiled and I thought 'Thank you, thank you God.' Carol joined us and we walked into the church together. There is a photograph that was taken of us somewhere in the attic. Outside the church, after the ceremony, David was enveloped by family and friends. They all wanted to know what he was up to and some, I'm sure, just wanted to be seen with him, now that he was world famous. Carol linked arms with me as we walked down the path.

'Are you okay?' she asked wearing her concerned look.

I'm fine. Why shouldn't I be?' I replied walking swiftly towards Mr Gravel, my old music teacher. I didn't see David again until we were at the reception. Naturally he sat on the top table with the bride and groom's families. I could feel his eyes seeking mine from time to time and his smile made me melt inside. This was supposed to have been the occasion when I would realise that David was happy with his wife and I would eradicate him from my mind and try to get on with the rest of my life but all my well intended plans were abandoned and I had a foreboding that the day would end with me feeling as dejected as ever. I tried to concentrate on the speeches – some of them were quite amusing. David then got up on his feet and apologised for the absence of his wife. He centred his speech on how good it was to be surrounded by family and friends on home turf and its importance to all of us. He continued by saying that marriages needed the support of a close network of friends and family you loved. I was wondering if he was trying to tell me something or was I hoping against hope that his marriage to Isabella was not the fairytale everybody was led to believe. The cake was duly cut and champagne was drunk. Everything was going well and everybody was enjoying the occasion.

There was a break of about two hours between the wedding reception and the evening party. Some of the guests, who lived nearby, slipped home for a couple of hours, others, staying at the hotel, went up to their rooms for a rest. Carol and I decided to have a pot of tea in the lounge before Carol went to her room and I decided to go for a walk in the grounds. I had taken it for granted that David had gone home with his parents but as I turned the corner into the rose garden I saw him sitting on a bench as if he was waiting for me. My heart missed a beat.

'I knew you'd come,' he said.

'How could you? I didn't even know you were still here. I thought you'd gone home with your family.'

He looked at me with a mischievous smile, 'Yes but we've always worked by telepathy. Come and sit down here. The scent from these roses is wonderful.'

'What if somebody sees us?'

'What's wrong with two old friends sitting and talking together?'

I sat down nervously because I didn't think people would see it like that. On the other hand I couldn't resist him. We did talk - about ourselves, what we'd been doing recently, talked about our families, talked about anything and everything except how we felt about one another. Gradually the non-stop chatter dwindled to a halt. We looked at each other and David squeezed my hand. I felt as if I was suffocating. I should have got up and left immediately but I didn't want to abandon him. All I wanted was to be in his company, to feel his touch, to drown in those lovely brown eyes and never go away again. David broke the silence.

'Perhaps we should go for a walk,' he said.

I could only nod, following him down the steps and moving as if in a dream, towards the wooded area at the bottom of the lawn. We were now completely hidden from any prying eyes from hotel bedroom windows. David drew me towards him, gently at first, but then the passion between us took over and it was as if we had never been apart. We were hungry for one another. I felt his strong arms wrap themselves around me and I pressed myself along his slim, toned body. This was ecstasy. He showered me with kisses, on my face, neck and then I felt his hand opening my dress zip. I stopped him.

I whispered, 'David we have to stop this – it's insane.'

'You were always the strong one weren't you Miss Goody Two Shoes?' he laughed, 'but I know you want to as much as I do.'

'Of course I do,' I replied. 'David, things aren't that simple are they? We're both married and imagine the effect on your career if anybody found out.'

'Beth, this isn't how it should have been. We were always meant for each other.'

I tried to be wise. 'That's how life turns out sometimes. Surely we shouldn't make things more complicated than they already are.'

'Is that your head or your heart talking?' he asked.

'You know me too well, that's the trouble,' I sighed.

 'Please,' he implored, 'just one more kiss before we go back and face the <u>hoards.</u>'

We melted into each other's arms and I wanted that kiss to last forever. We took separate paths up to the hotel and I went to the lounge to look for Carol. There was nobody I knew around and when I glanced at myself in the large mirror over the fireplace, I realised that I should go and tidy myself as my hair had escaped the carefully tied ribbons and I looked rather flushed. I had very little time to put things to rights before Carol knocked at my door.

'God, Beth,' she said, I was thinking of sending a search party to look for you. Where on earth have you been?' I explained that I'd walked further than I had intended and the paths were much steeper than I had anticipated.

'That's why you look so hot and bothered. Never mind, you've got about ten minutes to get ready. I'll see you in the foyer.' It took me about half an hour to calm down and get in the right frame of mind to meet people. When I felt able to face the world again, the party was warming up nicely. Carol was sitting down at one of the tables around the dance floor. She had probably got tired of waiting for me. She was talking to some girls who used to be in school with us so I joined them. It was then that I saw him. David was dressed semi casually in a light coloured suit with a plum coloured polo neck sweater underneath the jacket. He looked so handsome dancing there with Anita, his sister. I danced with one or two men whom I'd known for years and once with David's father. He asked me how life was treating me and seemed to know everything about the successful business Carol and I owned. He also asked me if I'd had the opportunity to talk to David as we used to be so close. I told him we'd only had a few words but perhaps I could catch up with him before the end of the evening. Hywel Meredith was such a nice man. Carol and I went in search of the buffet because David had been commandeered for most of the night. Much later, when I felt my last chances of seeing him again were slipping away, David made a bee line for me and dragged me on to the dance floor. The band was playing 'Unchained Melody,' one of my favourites, as we danced easily together. I was conscious of his closeness, his arm tightening around my waist, his hand gripping mine and more than anything his warm breath passing through my hair. There was no need for words. Both of us knew what the other was thinking. The music stopped but we still stood together oblivious of everybody and everything. The band struck up another waltz and we continued to dance. I had to break the spell as I suddenly became aware of people's eyes focusing on us. I panicked.

'David we must stop, people are talking about us.'

'Just let them. I don't want to stop, do you?'

'No, I mean yes. Oh God I don't know what I mean anymore.'

'Come on cariad, calm down or we really shall be the talk of the town. Beth, listen to me. I have to be back in London tomorrow but I'm staying the night here in the hotel because the aunts are stopping over with Mam and Dad.' We carried on dancing as he spoke quietly,

'My room number is 104. I'll be going up soon, pretending that I'm exhausted so I'll be courteously taking leave of the guests. You my darling will stay down here until at least midnight, then feign a headache and making sure nobody sees you, join me in my room.' I was shaking with anticipation, excitement, nervousness or whatever it was but I knew in my heart of hearts that I would do as he wished.

'Will you please Beth? Just this one night?' My eyes filled with tears as I looked up at him. I nodded as I was too choked to talk and his face lit up with an amazing smile.

'I want to shout out for the entire world to hear me.'

'For goodness sake, don't you dare,' I laughed. Before we parted he whispered,

'See you later.' I smiled and went back to Carol and the crowd and David went over to ask his mother to dance. It was about a quarter to eleven when David came over to our table to say goodnight. I hoped the others hadn't noticed the secret look he gave me as he kissed my cheek. Carol whispered something in his ear which made him laugh.

'What was all that about,' I ventured to ask.

'Mind your own business, nosey. Just a private joke between David and me,' she said slyly. We laughed but I felt a little uneasy. It was just after midnight that I started complaining of a headache. As I was prone to migraines everybody suggested I call it a day and go up to my room out of the noise. I couldn't believe that deception could be so easy. I did firstly go up to my room in order to gather enough courage to carry out the next step of the plan. I took the lift up to the second floor. Luckily there was nobody around as they were all enjoying themselves downstairs. I then took off my high heeled shoes so that I could run across the corridor in virtual silence. Finding David's room was more difficult than expected as it was on its own down a small passageway but at least that made it more private. By the time I knocked on the door I was flushed and out of breath. When David opened it he exclaimed,

'You look as if you've murdered someone and you're running from the scene of the crime.'

'No,' I replied, 'I'm running right into it.' We laughed and fell easily into each other's arms as David kicked the door shut.

'I've got a bottle of champagne on ice, would you like some?'

'Not now,' I replied, 'I've got much better things to do.'

'You shameless hussy. Come here you lovely, lovely girl.'

It was all so natural. There were no inhibitions. We were soul mates. We didn't have sex together, we made love and there is a vast difference between the two. We both wanted to please each other. We kissed, we laughed, we teased and we hungered for each other. Every moment together was special. Tongues teasing, skin against skin, hands clasping, eyes gazing, lips smiling. It was sheer ecstasy for both of us. I always knew it would be that good – we just fitted together perfectly.

Afterwards, we lay there for a long time not wishing to move.

'That champagne must be warm by now,' David whispered. 'Shall I get you some?'

'Well if you insist,' I said as I watched his taut body crossing the room. He really was so beautiful to look at. Even then I couldn't believe that I could still attract him.

'You seem miles away, cariad. What were you thinking about?'

I answered, 'Oh, lots of things. How much I've missed you and how I want tonight to go on forever.'

'Don't let's waste time being sad, Beth, we've got about five hours yet.'

We snuggled up together, sipping champagne, occasionally touching and kissing. What was even lovelier than the actual lovemaking was the cuddling whilst we dozed. I woke up just after six and propped myself up on my elbow and looked down on his sleeping face. I thought if only I had been brave enough to follow him I could have had all that for the rest of our lives together but it was too late for regrets. David opened his eyes and looked up at me smiling.

'Couldn't you sleep?' he asked drowsily.

'I was afraid of wasting any of the time we had together.'

He pulled me to him and we made love slowly and gently. There was something very sad and poignant about it as we both knew that we would have to say goodbye soon. I was determined not to cry when I left him. We hugged in silence and I fled down the corridor without a backward glance. I got into my room safely and I cried and cried. I then tried to make myself look presentable and went down to the dining room for breakfast with a lot of the other wedding guests including Carol.

I'll leave it there for now. I can only hope, Ceri, that you'll experience love like that someday. If you do, follow him wherever he takes you. Don't be foolish like I was and lose the opportunity of making a life together.

Love as always

Mamx

It was quite late that night when Beth finished writing her letter. She called David hoping that he'd arrived home. He sounded tired when he answered but perked up on hearing Beth's voice. He was very pleased that

Ceri had gone to the party but wished he could have been in Tŷ Cerrig to keep Beth company. Beth told him what she had been writing about in her current letter. David commented,

'I hope you didn't tell her too much – it could be embarrassing.'

Beth laughed, 'Only enough to make her realise how fantastic we were together and how special our relationship was.'

'You seem to be talking in the past tense, aren't we good together now?'

'Of course we are, silly – we always have been and always will be made for each other. Now go to bed and get some sleep, you sound tired. I love you more now than ever.'

'Me too,' said David, 'me too.'

Chapter 18

Beth heard a car turn up at about eleven o'clock on the Sunday morning. It was Ceri arriving. She had expected a phone call from her daughter asking her to pick her up from Donna's but evidently Steffan had borrowed his mother's car to bring her home. Beth thought she spied a kiss passing between them but she couldn't be sure. Ceri bounded into the house, smiling so Beth presumed that the party had gone well. Her daughter announced that she'd had a fantastic time and Donna's parents had wanted her to stay for Sunday lunch but she'd decided to come home in case her mother was lonely. Beth was quite touched. However, Ceri was going out again that the evening.

'Can I ask with whom?' Beth ventured.

'Steffan,' was the reply. 'Okay Mam, I really like him and he's fun to be with.'

'How long's he home for?'

'Six weeks, so he'll be going back to Australia just before I hope to get back to work. We'll see how things go. He'll probably get fed up with me way before then.'

Steffan did not tire of Ceri and they saw as much of each other as was possible. Beth was worried that his departure would have an adverse effect on Ceri's health and she'd be back to square one again but David told her not to worry so much and to let the young couple enjoy each other's company whilst they could. David managed to come down to Cwm Rhedyn for a couple of days during Steffan's stay and was very impressed with Ceri's friend and could see that the two young people enjoyed each other's company very much. Later that night, David ventured to mention,

'I think perhaps those two are becoming quite close.'

'Yes I know but I'm worried what's going to happen when he goes back to Sydney and Ceri's still in London.'

'If they really want to be together, they'll find a way.'

Beth looked at him and said, 'That makes me think that our love wasn't strong enough for us to be together.'

'I don't think that at all,' replied David. 'It wasn't as easy to keep in touch in our day. Think - there's e-mail, Facebook and Skype and they can use mobile phones for calls and text messages. They don't know how fortunate they are. Let's just see what happens, shall we?'

'What if Ceri moves to Australia?'

'I think we're getting ahead of ourselves a bit,' laughed David. 'I'm however very glad that our daughter is so much better and if that means she moves to Australia, so be it.' Beth was very subdued when they went to bed so David held her close so that she knew he'd always be there for her, come what may. When David returned to London and Ceri was spending most of her time with Steffan, Beth found she had time on her hands so filled it by writing her letters. She planned to finish them soon, as she really wanted Ceri to start reading them now that she wasn't so antagonistic towards David. Their relationship had carried on much as it had been when Ceri thought of David as her godfather but Beth noticed subtle changes – the way Ceri sought his approval, the way she listened to his opinion and her gradual acceptance of his and her mother's situation. David had been very careful not to try to usurp Alun's position and both he and Beth had not made their relationship public as it was much too soon after Alun's death. Carol called the day after David had gone home just to see how things were. Beth told her friend she was worried where

Ceri's relationship was going with Steffan being so far away. Carol knew Beth so well and said to her,

'I know what's going on in your mind. You're afraid your daughter will go flitting off to Australia. Listen Beth, it's early days yet and even if she does decide to go some day, don't you dare try and stop her or they could be in the same position as you and David have been all these years.'

Beth didn't argue because she knew that Carol spoke the truth so decided to make them some coffee instead of arguing. Over the next few days Beth spent time in the study writing.

Ceri, cariad,

The story continues:

During breakfast at the hotel after Anita's wedding, I was very quiet so Carol asked me what was wrong. I said there was nothing the matter but she knew me too well so in the end I confessed.

'My God girl, do you know what you're doing? David hinted to me last night what he was planning but I never thought you'd have the guts to go through with it. I'm not standing in judgement as I feel so sorry for both of you. You should always have been together. Well, what happens now?'

'Nothing.'

'Nothing, what do you mean?' She seemed surprised.

'David goes back to his wife and I go back to Alun and carry on as we have done. We're not going out to hurt people. This is our problem and we have to manage it. If I never spend time alone with David again, I can live on the memories of last night.'

'But Beth, surely you want more?'

'I'd love to have more but it's not possible. I'll take what I can get and be grateful for it. I don't expect you to understand but that's how it is. By the way,' I giggled, 'I'm absolutely shattered.'

Carol laughed. 'Was it that good then?'

'Better, much better.'

We escaped from the hotel before many of the guests had even woken up. I didn't want the pain of seeing David and not being able to kiss him goodbye.

Alun arrived home later that afternoon and before even taking his bag upstairs asked me,

'Well how was the wedding?'

'As weddings go it was very nice,' I replied, not wanting to go into much detail.

'Nice, what sort of word is that?

'Well, it all went very well. The bride was beautiful, the food was wonderful, what more do you want me to say?'

'So you enjoyed yourself then?'

'Yes, yes I did,' I replied starting to get a little uneasy at all the questioning.

He continued. 'Many people you knew there?'

'Yes, most of them but I sat with Carol and we joined up with some girls we knew from school, during the evening party.'

'That's all right then,' he said as if my answers had satisfied him and then took his things upstairs as I called out to him

'How was your trip?'

'Good,' he called back, 'but I'm really tired. I'm getting too old for these jaunts'

Mam came over to the house later to ask me about the wedding. She quizzed me about who I was with, what we did and of course, was David there and did I have a chance to talk to him. I answered her questions as near to the truth as possible but I didn't mention that David was at the wedding alone.

It was a few weeks after Anita's wedding that I started having heartburn and then a few days later the nausea started. Instinctively I knew what was wrong with me. I panicked because I really didn't know what to do. I didn't say a word to anybody for a while but one day, my mother came in to the shop and looked at me,

'You're looking a little peaky, love, anything wrong?'

'No Mam, it's just been one of those days.' I closed my eyes tightly for a moment, trying to quell the bout of nausea building up inside me.

'Beth, you really don't look at all well. Let's sit down and have a cup of tea. The girls can manage the shop. I went out into the fresh air when she prepared the tea. We sat together in the little storeroom at the back of the shop and she took my hand in hers,

'If there's anything worrying you, Beth, you know you can tell me don't you?' I nodded, another bout of nausea overwhelming me. Taking a deep breath, I blurted,

'I'm pregnant.'

'Mmm, I thought you were. We women have a sixth sense where these things are concerned. That's fantastic news love. Have you told Alun yet? He'll be thrilled.'

'No, I haven't because I need to get used to the situation first.' It had shocked me when Mam automatically assumed it was your father's. I knew it couldn't be his because we hadn't done anything that could make me pregnant for a long while. I continued,

'I'd like the doctor to confirm it first. I don't want Alun to get all excited and then find out it's a false alarm.' My mother gave me a strange look,

'Fine if that's how you want to play it but as you're evidently going to be somebody that has morning sickness, you'd better tell him soon or he'll start thinking that all manner of awful things are wrong with you.'

I hadn't thought of that. Alun as yet hadn't suspected anything but I had no idea how I was going to hide things from him. Probably the stress of the situation made me run and throw up in the toilet at the moment when Carol came through from the catering kitchen.

'God Beth what's up, you look terrible?'

'Must have eaten something. I'd better get home, I think, because it's best not to touch food in case I've caught some stomach bug.'

Carol walked me home and sat with me for a while. She offered to make me a cup of coffee but when she saw the look of repulsion on my face, she turned to me and said,

'Okay, madam, you may be able to kid the rest of the world but not me. You're pregnant aren't you?' I couldn't deny it.

'How long?'

'I don't know for sure if I am yet because it's too soon to see the doctor.' (We weren't into pregnancy testing kits back then.) I could see Carol thinking and probably making mental calculations.

'My God Beth!' She didn't need to say any more. 'Does anybody else know?'

'Yes Mam. She guessed actually but she's taken it for granted that it's Alun's and wants me to tell him soon.'

Carol continued, 'And could it possibly be Alun's?'

'No he hasn't done anything lately to make it possible, but he will.'

'Oh no, Beth you wouldn't?'

'I have to, Carol, I don't have any other choices.'

'You could tell David.'

'No definitely not. I am not going to ruin his career and his marriage – I love him too much. I cannot break Alun's heart and I know he will be absolutely thrilled that we're expecting a baby at last. I've made up my mind, Carol – I have to pass this baby off as his.' Before we had time to continue the discussion, Alun arrived home and was surprised to see the two of us there. Carol piped in,

'Beth had a slight migraine so I came home with her to make her a cup of tea. Do you want one Alun?' Your father was accustomed to me having migraines which included feelings of nausea so he wasn't overly concerned and encouraged me to go upstairs and rest. This was when my mind went to overdrive. I had to seduce Alun somehow and I knew that I'd have the perfect opportunity the following Saturday as the Golf Club were holding their annual awards dinner to which partners were invited. Quite a lot of alcohol would be consumed so I hoped he'd be in a frisky mood. I dressed with the utmost care that evening in a rather sexy, strappy dress. Alun looked stunned when he saw me in it.

'Wow, every man is going to be jealous of me tonight,' I smiled and felt pleased with myself. I made sure he didn't drink so much that he was incapable of performing and when we travelled home in the taxi, I snuggled right up to him so that I got him in the right mood. When we arrived home I pulled him up the stairs, took off my dress and said,

'Let's make a baby.' I didn't have to ask a second time. The difference between having sex with Alun rather than David was that there was no spontaneity, no reckless abandonment, and no soaring heights of passion. With Alun I always felt awkward and even a little shy but he seemed to be enjoying himself and was fulfilled at the end of it.

After kissing me on the cheek, he turned on his side and went to sleep but at least the deed had been done. I lay awake for hours thinking about what I was conjuring but I convinced myself that I was giving Alun something he wanted and I knew by doing so I was getting myself out of a very tight corner. I was aware that I would have to live with the consequences for the rest of my life.

I had cleverly managed to hide my nausea and sickness from your father but about three weeks after we had had sex he heard me heaving in the bathroom.

'Beth,' he said, 'I'm worried about you, I heard you being sick the day before yesterday as well and you are looking very pale. Perhaps you aught to visit the doctor.'

'Yes I think I shall,' I replied, but I have a feeling that I know what he will say.'

'What do you mean?'

'Think,' I said, 'Why do women throw up in the morning?

His reaction was really very funny and if the situation hadn't been so serious I would have burst out laughing. Firstly he looked puzzled and then it dawned on him and

to my amazement he punched the air and shouted, 'Yippee!'
It was all so out of character. He then grabbed me and
twirled me round and round until I felt quite sick. Well, I
thought, at least he was pleased.

'Beth, this is such marvellous news. Have you seen the
doctor?'

'Hold on,' I managed to say, 'I'll make an appointment
tomorrow to get it confirmed. We'll have some idea of dates
and then we'll be able to tell people. He seemed perfectly
happy with that arrangement and went off to prepare for
school with a silly grin on his face. I would have to think
very carefully about the dates so that neither Mam nor
Alun would be suspicious.

'Don't you dare tell anybody yet,' I shouted as he jumped in
the car. Of course the doctor confirmed that I was pregnant –
about eight weeks as I had already worked out. Fortunately
men weren't so involved in women's pregnancies in those
days so Alun hadn't visited the doctor with me, enabling
me to tell him that I had only gone a few weeks and my
mother was told that I was about six weeks pregnant so that
the baby wouldn't be too premature if it was born on time. It
was easier to kid your father than my mother who seemed
to be able to see inside my head. I asked him to keep the
news to himself for a while so that the pregnancy had time
to settle. In actual fact I needed other people to think I was
two months pregnant when they were told because a doctor
could rarely confirm it until six weeks had passed. It was
so complicated. So, poor Alun had to endure his secret for
a whole month. Mam wanted to know if I'd told him and
seemed puzzled that I had told him not to tell anybody. I

worried that she would let it slip that I had gone further into the pregnancy than Alun realised. The stress of it all was not helping my condition. When at last the news came out everybody was genuinely pleased for us as we had waited such a long time for this, our first baby.

One evening when Alun was in a Parent/Teacher meeting at the school, there was a knock on the front door. I hurried to answer it and there to my amazement stood David. I was transfixed and speechless as he took me in his arms and kissed me passionately.

'I couldn't stay away after that fantastic night we spent in that hotel. You're all I want, Beth. I think about you night and day. I love you so much,' he said.

'Stop,' I shouted. 'This whole situation is crazy, David.' I walked through into the kitchen and he followed me. 'We have to talk,' I said. It was wrong of us to have done what we did when we last met because we are both married and if we're going to survive, we have to let each other go.'

David held my hand (which I should have taken away) and told me,

'This is your prepared speech. This isn't the real you talking. Come on Beth, how could you kiss me as you did a few minutes ago and then make me think you want to spend the rest of your life with somebody else? It's senseless.'

I told him how I thought that the whole situation was idiotic. I also commented on the fact that he never mentioned his wife and the feelings they had for each other. He explained that he and Isabella got on primarily because they shared the same sort of life but they gave each other a free reign to do what they wanted.

'So she knows all about me then, does she?' I asked.

'Of course not.' answered David a little sheepishly.

'So it is deception David, it's not fair on her and definitely not fair on me.' I continued, 'As you said, you married somebody who fitted into your way of life. Don't you realise I've done exactly the same thing?'

'But I only did it because you wouldn't come into my life, Beth,' he said dolefully.

'I admit to that, but we've been through the reasons why, time and time again. That's all in the past and we need to move on.' I got up to make us some tea and I tried to pluck up the courage to tell him my very important piece of news.

'David.'

'Mmm?'

'I'm pregnant.'

The silence was tangible. The pain I saw in his eyes was unbearable. It was as if I had struck him.

'David, please say something,' I whispered.

'What is there left to say except that I wish you, your husband and your baby a happy life together?' Tears welled in my eyes,

'It's not like that. Listen to me David. It's not that simple.'

'I don't want to listen to any more,' he said with such pain in his voice. He then stopped and looked at me and suddenly something dawned on him,

'Oh God, Beth, please say it's not true.' We were both crying by now. 'It's my baby isn't it?'

'Yes my darling, it's yours,' I said through my tears.

He wanted to know why I was therefore staying with Alun and I explained that as he wasn't free to marry me, and I couldn't cart a small baby around the world's opera houses, I was going to be practical and give the child the best life possible under the circumstances.

'Alun's a good man and he'll make an excellent father. He already knows about the baby and is absolutely thrilled.'

'I don't care if he's a bloody saint,' shouted David. 'It's my baby in there,' he cried, placing his hand possessively on my stomach.

'Don't David, don't,' I wailed. 'This is sheer hell as it is, so please don't make it any worse. The baby will be brought up as Alun's and he or she will never know the truth. Your career is going from strength to strength so don't jeopardise it with this sort of scandal. The world owns you my love. Don't disappoint people.' We just held each other tightly not wishing to let go. The final blow came when he said,

'Just for the record, Isabella can't have children.'

I felt as if I'd been punched in the stomach. At that moment I heard Alun arriving home. He was full of the joys of spring with a bottle of champagne in his hand.

'Look what the staff bought me,' he called out. It was a second before he noticed David standing by the sink. He crossed the kitchen to shake his hand and there they stood chatting amicably together – my world famous lover and my nice, ordinary husband. After a while Alun suggested we tell David our secret.

'We're so pleased about it because we've waited so long,' continued Alun.

David retorted, 'I'm very jealous of you because my wife is barren.' How I hated that word and in the light of the circumstances it was doubly horrible. Alun was very sympathetic but David told him that it was just bad luck and said it wouldn't have been an ideal lifestyle to bring up a child. Alun, as if to sever the awkward conversation, opened the bottle of champagne and he and David drank a toast to the forthcoming baby. I looked on trying to hide my emotions. I wanted to scream because in a way I knew it was entirely my fault and nothing would convince me otherwise.

Out of the blue (I'm not sure if it was the drink talking) Alun announced,

'I've just had the most splendid idea.' I held my breath.

He turned to David and said, 'You can be our baby's godfather. Don't you think that's a brilliant idea, Beth? David can have a sort of share in our child as he can't have one of his own.' I was flabbergasted and David looked stunned.

Alun continued, 'You'll be doing us a great honour, David. Imagine our little one will be able to boast about his or her famous godfather. You can visit us any time you're over in this country.' I felt as if I was dying on the spot and David only managed to stutter something inaudible which Alun took as a 'yes.' So that was the beginning of my very strange, complicated relationship with two men.

Well Ceri I feel rather drained by all that. I hope you realise I did try to do things for the right reasons even if you blame me for the decisions I made.

Mam xxx

Beth went to bed early that night as reliving that particular so period of her life, even after many years, had exhausted her.

Chapter 19

Beth busied herself around the house for the next couple of weeks. She tidied the garden, washed some curtains and gave the utility room a much needed coat of paint. She saw very little of Ceri, whose state of mind, had improved beyond recognition due to the effects of Steffan on her life. Ceri's doctor was satisfied that she could return to work soon so she and Steffan decided to spend a week together in London before his return to Australia. This would give them a chance to sample a few of the sights and get Ceri back into city life before she started her work in earnest. David was thrilled with their decision as he'd been feeling rather lonely in the large apartment on his own. Beth on the other hand decided to stay in Cwm Rhedyn until Steffan's departure, thinking that Ceri would probably need her more in London then.

Ceri tried not to cry when Steffan left but the way they clung to each other signified that this had been more than a holiday romance. David gave Ceri some space for the next two days and then encouraged her to go over to the theatre to discuss her return to work. Beth arrived that evening and was pleasantly surprised to see a very buoyant, positive Ceri. David informed Beth that there had been a lot of phoning and 'Skyping' but Ceri seemed to be managing things very well and was planning to go back to work the following week, agreeing to start back in the chorus and take it from there. This would give her time to see if she could cope with the pressure. Beth aimed to stay up in London for three weeks as she loved having David and her daughter close but as the period drew to a close, she yet again pined for Wales and her home in Cwm Rhedyn. David planned to travel back with her and spend a couple of days unwinding in the peace and quiet of rural life. He talked about his retirement again and said he had definitely decided to withdraw from the operatic circuit within the six months. He would remain in his current role as Cavaradossi in Puccini's Tosca at Covent Garden until the powers- to- be decided on his replacement. He had already started discussions about his plans with his agent and they had had meetings with the musical director and everybody else concerned. David explained to Beth that the last thing he wanted to do was go and on until his voice was second class. He wanted people to remember him at the top of his game. He also wanted to spend more precious time with her and his daughter, if Ceri allowed him. They discussed what they would do with the house in Cwm Rhedyn and the apartment in the city once more. Again they came to the conclusion that the best course of action for the immediate future was to keep them both as David needed the buzz of London and its amenities whereas Beth wanted to be near her Welsh roots and familiar surroundings. They decided they would come and go as they chose, either together or sometimes apart, which would give the relationship time to breathe and develop. Nobody except Ceri and Carol knew there was anything between them other than friendship and they meant to keep it that way for a while. Beth wanted to continue her work with the local choir and David, being a patron of The Royal Opera House, Covent Garden decided to look for additional ways of becoming involved. He also wanted to set up some sort of scholarship connected to The Royal National Eisteddfod of Wales – something that would enable young Welsh people to follow their musical dreams as he had. David had already travelled the world, mainly through his work but he wanted to show Beth some of the amazing places he had seen as she had never been outside of Europe. Carol thought their planning for the future was very wise and she surprised them both by announcing her own bit of news. She had been offered a very favourable price for her business which she was seriously considering as it would enable her, also, to do some of the things she had on her wish list. So the three friends discussed their future over a decent bottle of wine – not now the distant dreams of teenagers but ones of people in their sixties hoping they would be around long enough to see them reach fruition.

It surprised David how quickly the Press sniffed out his plan to retire. It wasn't that he minded people knowing but it did make his intent more definite and with that came the realisation that his life would be very different. He was excited by the prospect but also a tad apprehensive. Beth's life carried on as normal as her daily life wasn't going to change all that much. She wondered if people would accept her relationship with David when it was made public. She genuinely worried about Alun's mother finding out as she had recently been very ill suffering from some severe chest infections which could have easily developed into pneumonia. Elsie Rees was ninety-three years old and had become very frail. Any major trauma could affect her health so Beth did not want her mother-in law to know about her and David. Even though the two women had never hit it off, Beth couldn't be that heartless. She also worried that the old lady would put two and two together and somehow work out that Ceri wasn't her son's child. Although this notion was ridiculous Beth didn't want anything to spoil Ceri's relationship with her *Mamgu*. David told Beth not to be such a worrier and as long as they were careful neither Alun's mother nor anybody else would be become aware of their situation until they decided the time was right.

Whilst Beth spent time in Cwm Rhedyn she decided to finish her letters to Ceri so she persuaded herself to spend time in the study, each morning in order to complete the job.

Ceri, cariad,

At last I can actually see an end to this saga so I'm hurtling towards the finishing line as quickly as I can.

The pregnancy was settling down and I was feeling less sick in the mornings and was able to do my work in the shop. The outside catering part of the business was really taking off and Carol was run off her feet. We decided to split the work in half – I was in charge of the shop and everything that went with it and Carol oversaw the catering section. We met once a week so that we were both 'au fait' with each other's work schedule. We also worked on joint accounts so that each part of the business benefited from the other. Bara Menyn had been a great triumph and we were both immensely proud of our achievements. It was miraculous that we never quarrelled but I'm sure this was probably the key factor to our success.

One busy morning at work I suffered some stomach cramps. I didn't think much of it at first, until I went to the toilet and saw spots of blood – nothing much but enough to make me panic. I went over to tell Carol and she immediately propelled me unceremoniously into the back of her car and took me straight to the hospital. I was told to relax and they strapped me on to a monitor. Later they gave me an ultrasound scan (this wasn't a normal procedure back then) to make sure you were okay. Mercifully the bleeding stopped and no harm had been done but it did give me an awful fright because I wanted my baby so much. I was convinced I was being punished for what I had done. Carol contacted Alun and he had dashed over as soon as he could. He was naturally worried but the doctor tried to allay our fears by convincing us that these little blips occurred from time to time. I was told I needed more rest as my blood pressure was too high and would need constant monitoring throughout the pregnancy. I had to stay in the hospital for two days as a precautionary measure which I didn't mind if it meant I could carry my baby safely. Unbeknown to me, Carol had also managed to get in touch with David in his hotel in Berlin. I was sitting on the bed waiting for Alun and my mother to come to take me home when I saw David rushing across the ward towards me.

'Oh God!' I thought. It wasn't that I didn't want to see him but how on earth was I going to explain his being there to Mam and Alun. The poor man had flown from Berlin directly after he had heard what had happened and urged me to tell him exactly what had taken place and what the doctors had to say. He hugged me and I clung to him but couldn't relax as I knew we wouldn't be alone for very long. I assured David that I was alright and no harm had been done to our baby. I had to promise him faithfully that I would do everything the doctors told me to and he also insisted that I write to him every week so that he felt part of the pregnancy and he would send replies to Carol's house if and when he could. At that moment Alun and my mother arrived. They both looked surprised to see David there but he expertly defended himself saying that he was just visiting his parents overnight because he had a couple of days free from work. He said that he had bumped into Carol in town an hour or so earlier and decided to pop in to visit me quickly to see how I was getting on. Alun seemed satisfied with the explanation and said jokingly,

'You have to keep an eye on your forthcoming godchild don't you?'

'Of course,' replied David equally light-heartedly.

Mam looked puzzled but didn't mention it again until she was alone with me.

'It seems very odd to me that you've asked David to be the baby's godfather.'

I told her the story and it sounded so much better that Alun had asked him and not me. Mam still wore her puzzled look. Sometimes I felt she could see exactly what was going on in my head.

It was a few weeks before David managed to get in touch with me again. He phoned me from New York when he knew I was at work and when I heard his voice, I burst into tears. Pregnancy made me over- emotional but David became very concerned and it took me ages to reassure him that expectant mothers could be very silly.

'I wish I could be with you,' he cried. 'I wish I could be there to feel the baby moving and to take care of you. Oh Beth, I'm missing you so much and I need to see you. It was unbearable at the hospital, not being able to touch you.'

'I know, I know,' I replied, 'but this is how it's going to be and somehow we've got to deal with it.'

'We must find a way of meeting – I'll have to think of something,' David said with desperation in his voice. He carried on talking like this and I began to realise that the situation was becoming unbearable. I wasn't sure how I was going to stand the stresses and strains of my double life and my blood pressure was continuing to be problematic. I tried to change the subject, asking about his work and New York but he wasn't going to be fobbed off so in the end I told him that Alun was going away on a residential course with his school, the following month. David was overjoyed because he was miraculously free at that time and would be in London. He sounded so excited,

'I'll think of something, Beth,' he promised. 'I'll phone you as soon as I arrive in London the week after next.' I wanted to ask him about Isabella but thought better of it. Most of the time I could blot her from my mind but occasionally her image floated past my psyche, which I found quite disconcerting. Occasionally during the following week Alun looked at me in a strange way and kept asking me if I was feeling alright because sometimes I looked preoccupied. I told Carol what was going on and my lovely partner- in- crime came up with a solution to our problem – that is our meeting place problem. She said that when David was in the area, we could meet at her house. This could be during the day when she was at work or in the evening when she was out somewhere. She even designated her spare bedroom for our use. It would be easy for me to find excuses to go over to Carol's and there was nothing odd in David paying his old friend a visit. This settled, I wrote to David to let him know of the plan. He was ecstatic and wrote back immediately saying that he couldn't wait to see me.

I was advised to give up work and I think your father was relieved because I was getting very tired and he was worried about the blood pressure business. Actually I never went back to the shop after you were born. I loved being at home with you and when you were still a baby I sold my half of the business to Carol. I didn't think I could cope with the stress of running a business and taking care of you and your father preferred to have his wife running the home rather than a business.

The plans for our meetings worked successfully and to make things appear kosher David always tried to visit us at Tŷ Cerrig or he would telephone and pretend he didn't have time to come over to Cwm Rhedyn on that particular visit. He only managed to come over to see me another twice during my pregnancy because of his hectic work schedules but it was enough to keep me buoyant. Both my men pampered me and both looked forward to the forthcoming birth. The problem with my blood pressure continued and about two weeks before my proper due date I was told that it would be better if I spent the remainder of the pregnancy in hospital as I had developed a condition known as pre-eclampsia. The doctor told me to go home and pack my bag because for my safety and the baby's I needed to be monitored and have complete hospital rest. He also told me to ask my mother if she had suffered from the same condition when she was expecting me. I was upset when I arrived home because I was worried about my baby and I didn't relish having to stay in hospital for two weeks. In one way it proved to be a blessing in disguise because it could be used as an excuse for bringing the birth forward so that nobody would question my exact birth date. When I was waiting for Alun to pick me up to take me back to the hospital, I remembered to ask Mam about the pre-eclampsia. I recall she was standing staring out of the kitchen window when I asked her and suddenly she became very quiet. She didn't utter a word for a while and then when she turned round I saw that she was crying.

'What on earth's the matter Mam?' I asked.

'I can't tell you about pre-eclampsia,' she said.

'Well it doesn't matter, it's not that important' I assured her. It was then that she told me,

'I can't tell you because I've never been pregnant.'

This was the very first time that I knew that I had been adopted. I was too stunned to say anything. At that same moment Alun came in and demanded to know what on earth had happened to me as I was as white as a sheet. He was terrified because all I kept shouting was,

'Take me away from this woman.' In the car I sat like a zombie and Alun drove like a maniac because he didn't know what was wrong with me and was worried sick. By the time the doctor saw me I was shaking uncontrollably and then I started to cry hysterically. The doctor asked Alun what had happened because it was evident I was going through some form of shock. Of course poor Alun was as puzzled as the doctor. When all this palaver was going on Carol arrived and she was able to shed some light on the matter as my mother had called her and explained the situation. I have never seen Alun so angry. He called my mother all names under the sun and said it would be her fault if anything happened to me or the baby. He would never forgive her for waiting until I was practically in labour before telling me. Thank goodness Carol was there to calm him down – she was good at that. Within the hour I started having contractions which had probably occurred as a result of the shock. Carol stayed with Alun until you were born about eight hours later. Miraculously it was a fairly straightforward birth and as you only weighed five pounds three ounces, people believed you were born prematurely. You had very dark hair which would have been

suspicious if I hadn't dark hair also. We stayed in hospital
for five days after the birth, which was the norm in those
days. I was besotted with you and so was Alun. I wouldn't
let my mother near you which must have distressed her a
great deal. Carol tried to persuade me to at least let her see
the baby but I wouldn't budge. When you were two days
old David bounced in to the hospital grinning like the
cat that got the cream with an enormous bouquet for me
(thank goodness he had the sense not to buy red roses) and
a gigantic teddy bear for you – of course you still have it
up in London. He fell in love with you instantly and the
way he cuddled and cosseted you made me feel so sad that
he would never have the chance to be your proper father.
He was shocked to hear my news about being adopted but
tried to persuade me that it wasn't the end of the world and
I should see my mother and talk some more with her. I was
adamant that I never wanted to see her again because I felt
I'd been deceived and I didn't like it. You see Ceri, I really do
understand what you've been through recently but you'll
find out as the story unfolds that Mam also acted with the
best of intentions. At least Ceri I am your natural mother
and you've known your natural father all your life. I'm so
sorry that I've just struck you another blow. I should have
told you this part of my story earlier.

Anyway when I arrived home with you, my mother was
waiting for us at Tŷ Cerrig. I was about to tell her to go but
Alun urged me to sit down and listen to what Mam had
to say before upsetting myself again. Alun left us alone
so that my mother could relate her story. She told me that
her younger sister, Doreen, became pregnant at seventeen.
The boy involved hadn't even been told for whatever reason
and she was left in a sticky situation. The two people I

knew as my mother and father had not been able to produce any children of their own so they decided to adopt Aunty Doreen's baby. My aunt was packed to an unmarried mother's home in the north of England until I was born and then my parents formally adopted me. Aunty Doreen stayed up near Newcastle and met Uncle Harry there. She never told him that she had had a baby. So in case I let the truth slip out I was never told the story of my adoption and the reason behind it. I suddenly realised why my Aunt had been so good to me over the years – baking special birthday cakes, helping me out at the shop so that I could take time off, supporting me when my father died and so on and of course making sure I didn't get close to David so that I wouldn't get hurt when he inevitably went away. Mam was willing to relate the story at that particular time because Uncle Harry was dead by then. I was sitting trying to digest all this information when Mam announced she was going home and as she was leaving she turned to me and said,

'Don't judge me too harshly, Beth. I'm not so different from you. I wonder if or when you'll tell your little girl who her real father is?' If she had slapped me across the face I wouldn't have been more shocked. I turned on my heels and left the room without any reply or argument which was probably enough to convince my mother that her assumptions were correct. The problem is Ceri, by protecting one person's feelings, you end up hurting another. That is certainly a lesson I've learnt in my life. You probably wonder why I never told you that I was adopted. I honestly don't know except that Aunty Doreen didn't want anybody to know the truth particularly her children from her marriage to Uncle Harry. So Ceri I'm imploring you not to tell anybody who *my real mother is, at least while she's still alive. I haven't even told David so that tells you how important this is to me. Although Aunty Doreen came to know that my mother had told me the truth, she has never mentioned it, so neither have I. It was that sort of era – things were pushed under the carpet and not talked about. It probably wasn't a good thing but that's how it was. I was given a jolt when you became pregnant and we found out about the hereditary disease in Matt's family. I wondered if any such disease, which I didn't know about, had been carried down through my father's line. It certainly made me think that perhaps I should have found out more about him.*

Well Ceri bach, I'm going to close for now. The next letter will be the last and I promise there will be no more shocks in it.

My fondest love

Mam xxxx

Beth sat in the study for a long time after writing the letter, mulling things over in her mind. She decided she would visit Aunty Doreen in the care home the following day as she felt it was her duty to find out more about her real father. She felt more content once her decision had been made. David phoned her late that night to confirm that Ceri was doing well at work and there had been some mention of her going back to take the lead part once again. Beth was thrilled and told him she'd be coming up to London soon because she was missing them both so much.

Chapter 20

Doreen was surprised but pleased to see her niece. It was a beautiful, sunny afternoon so Beth persuaded Aunty Doreen to walk with her in the care home's lovely gardens. They sat near the fish pond in the mellow, autumn sunshine. After the usual chit-chat, Aunty Doreen turned to Beth and said,

'Come on now Beth, I know you too well, you didn't come all the way to talk about the weather, did you?'

Beth nodded and decided to come straight to the point. She admitted to her aunt that she had known about her being her natural mother for years but she couldn't understand why they had never talked about it.

'Well Beth,' replied her aunt, 'I only gave birth to you; your mother was the one who gave you a happy home and looked after you faultlessly for all those precious years. I was fortunate to have access to your life but Harry, my husband, knew nothing about you. He understood that you had been adopted but had no inkling that you were my child. My own mother never spoke to me after I became pregnant – she was too ashamed of me. I was sent away to an unmarried mother's home in Newcastle and as I wasn't welcome at home I decided to stay in the area and get a job in a clothes shop. I met Harry; we got married and soon had both your cousins in quick succession. We didn't move to Llanelli until both my parents had passed away and by that time you were grown up and about to get married to your lovely husband, Alun. It was easier that way. My own mother never found out that my sister had adopted my child. I thought the world of my sister and would never have tried to take you away from her. I knew she'd told you the truth after Harry died but I, on the other hand, didn't want to discuss it as I didn't want anybody's life to change. Why bring unhappiness for no good reason?'

Beth listened attentively without interrupting but then added,

'What about now, Aunty Doreen, wouldn't you like me to think of yourself as my mother now?'

'Not really dear. I've never thought of you as my daughter – I didn't have the right to but I've always loved you as a very special niece.' Beth thought how different things had been for David – always wanting to be a real father to Ceri but not being allowed to.

'What about my cousins, don't you think they have a right to know that I'm their half sister?'

'That's up to you Beth but I'll ask you one favour. Please don't tell them while I'm still alive. I don't really want to know their reaction nor do I want to have to answer any of their awkward questions – not at my age.'

Beth nodded and promised yet again not to reveal her aunt's secret. She was relieved that she had warned Ceri in the letter not to mention the relationship to anybody. Before she had time to ask her aunt about her own father, Aunty Doreen got in first.

'I suppose you want me to tell you who your real father was, don't you?'

Beth tried to explain why she wanted to know that now. She related her daughter's story and how Ceri had to abort her baby because of the risk of a hereditary disease carried down through the male line of the father's family. Aunty Doreen listened carefully and sympathised but was adamant that she would never reveal the name of Beth's natural father. She said that everybody's life was a lottery and it was highly unlikely that there were any hidden illnesses to worry about. The only thing she was willing to disclose was that he was a good lad from a very decent family who had been too young to be a father at that time. She never blamed him. She hadn't told him about the pregnancy because it would have spoilt his life and blossoming career. This reminded Beth so much of her own predicament over the years, except that David did know about Ceri. Doreen warned Beth,

'Don't go looking for him love, you could upset and destroy many people's lives by doing so. He's isn't alive – I know that much so there's no point in raking up the past.' She then told her niece that she was very tired and needed to rest so the two women walked together arm in arm towards the house - both glad in a way that they had had the long overdue conversation.

Beth didn't tell David that she'd visited her aunt because he'd want to know why she'd gone there. Beth started to question herself why she had told Ceri the story in the letter – perhaps she aught to go back and re-write it. On the other hand she was trying to put things right by telling her daughter the whole truth. She would have liked to know more about her real father but in the circumstances decided she should probably let the past rest, at least for the moment, as her aunt wished. She started to wonder if David's mother and sister, Anita, aught to be told the facts about their relationship to Ceri. Perhaps, on second thoughts, those details should be put on hold for a while. On the other hand, David's mother was approaching ninety so time was of the essence. Beth's brain was racing and consequently getting very muddled. She then realised that if David's family got to know the truth, Alun's mother was bound to find out somehow and then there would be all hell to pay. It was all becoming very complicated. Beth hardly slept that night and was glad when Carol called at Tŷ Cerrig the following morning. Her friend's very buoyant mood rubbed off on Beth. Carol had come to announce that she had sold her business for an excellent price and she would be officially retiring at the end of the month. Beth forgot all her dilemmas for a while as they celebrated news. They even drank a whole bottle of champagne at eleven o' clock in the morning which resulted in Beth sleeping away the afternoon. When she eventually awoke it was getting dark and the house felt cold and spookily silent. Suddenly she felt very lonely so she decided on an impulse to pack her bag and go up to London the following morning.

Neither David nor her daughter was expecting her, so Beth entered the apartment with her own key and surprised them both when they returned from work late that evening. She had prepared a light supper for them all as she was sure neither would feel much like cooking after a long day's work. David was overjoyed to see her and hoped she would stay for a while because he missed her so much. Ceri went to her room after supper, primarily because she was exhausted but she wanted David and her mother to have some time alone together. She realised how much both of them came to life in each other's company and recognized that her mother had never been like that with her father. In some ways that hurt her but she was beginning to understand, through her own relationship with Steffan, what real love felt like. Beth questioned David about his forthcoming retirement and was pleased to learn that he'd be singing in his last stage appearance at Covent Garden two months later. She wanted to make sure that David had no reservations about his decision but after a great deal of quizzing him she felt he was absolutely comfortable with it. He was wise enough to make sure he had a few little projects up his sleeve to keep him adequately occupied but told Beth that the first thing he was going to do was to take her away to somewhere special and she could help him choose the destination. Of course Beth reminded him that if they went away together people would put two and two together about their relationship.

'Well,' retorted David, 'perhaps it's time we told certain people – my family for instance.'

Beth wore her worried look and she tried to explain how she hated the thought of Alun's mother hearing about it. David told her as gently as possible that they couldn't wait for everybody to die before their relationship became public because after all they weren't young themselves and needed to make the most of the time they had left. They decided they would tell David's mother when they were both next in Cwm Rhedyn and they would go to Cardiff for a week-end in order to tell Anita but they would let Alun's mother hear it along the grapevine. Beth felt uncomfortable about this but David tried to remind her how horrible the old woman had been to her for all the years she had been married to her son. Beth wanted to know if they should spill the beans about Ceri to David's family but he thought they should think very carefully before revealing all – probably that piece of news would be a step too far and he questioned whether the information would bring joy or hurt to people? It was lovely to cuddle up in each other's arms that night in the king-size bed realising that whatever happened they both belonged together and that this could happen every night if they so wished.

Ceri had slipped back into her role as Sophie in the musical Mama Mia seamlessly and was thoroughly enjoying herself except for the fact that Steffan was so far away. She was glad she was kept busy as it gave her less time to miss him. During Beth's stay in London Ceri confronted her with some news. Steffan had asked her to join him in Australia for a couple of week's holiday. Before saying yes, Ceri wanted to discover her mother's reaction. Beth told her she was delighted that things were progressing so well between them and that she should go without hesitation. Her mother also told her it would be a fabulous experience and she was not to worry about her because she had David and of course, Carol. David was also pleased that Ceri and Steffan seemed to be getting closer and surprised his daughter by saying he'd pay for her flight as an early birthday present so that she would only need to find her own spending money. Ceri was thrilled and came over and hugged him which brought tears to David's eyes. For the first time he hoped that there was a slight possibility that Ceri was starting to accept his new role in her life. Beth on the other hand felt annoyed with him because she couldn't possibly compete with that sort of gift. David could see from her expression that he'd done something wrong and when they had a minute alone asked her what he'd done to merit the cold shoulder treatment. Beth tried to explain that by giving Ceri such a generous gift, any of her own presents would seem paltry. David admitted that he hadn't stopped to think and said he understood where she was coming from and apologised for not discussing it with her first. Naturally as he had enough money he wanted to spoil his child but realised that from now on, if he wanted to be with Beth, everything was not about him and what he wanted.

One day David came home after morning rehearsals to spend some time with Beth. His agent had called him with an invitation to take part in Piers Morgan's Life Stories, a very probing television interview programme. David hadn't committed to anything because he needed to discuss it firstly with both Beth and Ceri. He underlined the fact that everything would be revealed if he went on the programme because Piers Morgan was very clever at getting people to divulge secrets.

'You're not going to do it are you?' implored a horrified Beth realising that everybody, in Cwm Rhedyn and beyond would get to know the whole story.

'Well I haven't said no. Perhaps it would be the best way to handle things,' replied David. 'Everything would be out in the open, - nothing to hide – no more secrets.' Beth wasn't at all sure and Ceri was afraid it would ruin her mother's reputation and also of course David's. They all decided to sleep on it and have a further discussion in the morning. Beth turned it over and over in her mind and in the end thought, 'What the Hell, let everybody know.' If individuals rejected her, so be it, because the people who really mattered would always be there for her. Ceri thought the whole thing could be fun - shocking David's opera buff fans and the puritanically inclined in Cwm Rhedyn. So she decided to tell David to go for it. Unanimously it was settled that David should take part in the programme. Beth would be invited to be present in the audience whereas Ceri, and Carol would take part in separate recorded interviews. The programme producers also wanted Anita, David's sister to take part so that pushed the plan about telling her their story, forward and Ceri's history would have to be part of the shock. The other thing that Beth needed to do was persuade Ceri to read her letters before she was questioned so that she would have a more balanced view of the situation. Beth made it clear to David that she did not want her own adoption mentioned as that was a private matter for her. He didn't really understand why she was so secretive and sensitive about it but told her not to worry on that score because they were investigating his life and not hers. They had about four months before the programme was due to be recorded so it gave them adequate time to get their house in order. Beth's priority was writing her last letter to Ceri, so the next day when David and her daughter were at work she took it on herself to complete her task.

Chapter 21

Dear Ceri,

Here I am sitting in the London apartment trying to fill in the gaps of your whole life as a child. Actually you probably remember most of it except for your earlier baby days, so I shall keep it as short as possible.

You were an easy baby and you had a lots of caring people around you. My mother and Aunty Doreen doted on you and were always there if I needed babysitters and your father idolised you, as he did for the rest of his life – your own memories should confirm this. Carol was fantastic, as usual and as your Godmother (and official caterer) arranged your Christening. David made sure he could attend as he had fully adopted his role of Godfather. I was very nervous but actually it proved to be a lovely day even though Mamgu insisted that you wore the hideous, family christening gown (which had turned a patchy yellow with age and had a few holes in the lace where the moths had been busy). Mamgu of course had to comment on the fact that David Meredith was your Godfather and not Alun's brother but I just bit my tongue and let the moment pass without explanation. I had very little time to see David on my own that day but he managed to tell me how thrilled and proud he was to have such a beautiful daughter and that he would always look out for us without ever upsetting the applecart. I was grateful for that and I began to feel a little more relaxed.

Time moved on and you grew to be a gorgeous little girl with your long, dark hair, which was the envy of people even in those days, and those dark brown eyes (which reminded me so much of David's). I kept in touch with David through occasional phone calls but mainly by letter. I sent him duplicates of as many photos of you as possible and he came back to Cwm Rhedyn as often as his schedule allowed. When we did manage to get together it always felt as if we'd never been apart. He'd often say that he wished he could be with us full time but if I'm honest, he wouldn't have liked the life we led. He would have missed his glittering career too much and would have become dissatisfied very quickly. I would then probably have blamed myself for spoiling his life – no it was not to be. His career was forever reaching new heights. I was immensly proud of him and even though I longed for him we managed to survive apart. I was fortunate to have found a good husband and an excellent father for you. He was always kind and considerate and I tried my best not to let him down because I was so grateful for everything he had given us. David arrived back for the big occasions in life – special birthdays and the time you were ill with appendicitis and my mother's funeral but it was Alun who was there for the everyday things. Sometimes I wonder if my relationship with David would have lasted through the struggles of day to day life. Perhaps I was lucky – I managed to keep the love of two very special men and you have been fortunate to have been at the receiving end of that devotion as well.

You grew up and started carving out a life for yourself with that same single-mindedness that I saw in David. You were always a great joy to my mother and I'm sure you'll agree that you had a very special relationship with her. I know we both felt a huge void in our lives when she died but as always Aunty Doreen made sure we were okay. We had a good life together, your father and I and I believe you had a happy childhood despite all the unknown facts – I hope so. We tried to do our best.

David and Isabella's marriage didn't last. They split up when you were about ten and later divorced. There was quite a bit about it in the press at the time. They said that Isobella couldn't live with such a cold-hearted man who always seemed to be in a different part of the world from where she was. The story sounded like a figment of somebody's imagination especially when they mentioned that David hadn't wanted children which added to their reasons for separating. I was annoyed that David hadn't put them straight but he didn't feel like making matters worse, so let it go and people forgot all about it very quickly. You probably wonder why we didn't get together then. The point was that you always had to come first – I was not going to spoil your life by uprooting you and dragging you to God knows where. Also you adored your father and I wasn't going to hurt either of you by being selfish. David sometimes asked me to re-consider but he knew in his heart of hearts that I wouldn't budge on that one so we continued as we were for all those years. At least we weren't upsetting anybody.

Well Ceri, my love, I've been as frank as I could in these letters. I hope you will not be too embarrassed when reading parts of them but to make sense of things, the whole story had to be told.

Difficult times will have to be faced when everybody gets to know about all this but remember, you had no part in that deception – that is something that David and I have to sort out. Stay strong my darling child.

All my love, always

Mam xxx

Beth felt very emotional when she put her pen down for the last time. In some ways writing the letters had sapped her energy but in others it had proved cathartic and even cleansing. When David returned that evening, he found her sitting in the gloom, yet looking serene and peaceful. He was sorry he had to disturb her by switching on the light but she turned to him with the loving smile that always tugged at his heart. She rose and slipped her arms around his neck and kissed him deeply before announcing that the letters were all ready for Ceri to read. David asked if he should take a look at them first but Beth shook her head vehemently. This was something between her and her daughter so David realised it would be best if he kept out of it. When Ceri arrived home late that night, Beth handed her the box containing the letters explaining that it would be wise to read them sooner rather than later especially with the Piers Morgan television programme looming. Ceri looked puzzled and a little wary but took them to her room, leaving Beth to speculate what would happen next.

A whole week passed without Ceri mentioning the letters. Beth wondered whether she should bring up the subject but decided not to appear pushy again. Then suddenly, out of the blue, when they were alone one day Ceri announced that she'd read the letters and it was a better read than a Jackie Collins novel. Beth wasn't sure how to react but Ceri laughed, 'Don't look so worried Mam but did you have to tell me all the gory details? I'm sure I'd have got the picture without you having to be quite so explicit! However they have made me understand a few things a bit clearer. Why didn't you tell me you were adopted and who your birth mother was before now?'

'Because Aunty Doreen didn't want Uncle Harry or her children to find out the truth – and she still doesn't. I haven't even told David because the more people who get to know, the more likely it is for the secret to come out. I've even promised Aunty Doreen that I'll not tell her children (my cousins) as long as she's alive, so please don't mention it to anybody.' Ceri nodded.

'The other thing is that I can't fathom how anybody could live for years and years with a man one didn't love,' commented Ceri, shaking her head in disbelief.

'There are many kinds of love, Ceri. I cared very deeply for your father and I miss him more than you'll ever know. David, on the other hand, was and is my soul mate – always has been and always will be. I've loved them both in different ways and both of them have truly loved you.' By this time, Beth was holding her daughter's hand and looking straight into her eyes, which were holding back the tears. They hugged and Ceri slowly let down the barriers, crying on her mother's shoulder until she was exhausted. Beth soothed her as she used to when Ceri was a small child. She persuaded her to lie on the settee with her head resting on the sumptuous cushions and Beth covered her with a throw and when David arrived home Beth placed her finger to her mouth ordering him to be quiet as Ceri had fallen asleep. They went through to the kitchen so that Beth could tell him what had happened but they were only half way through drinking a cup of coffee when Ceri came through to join them. They were afraid to say anything but Ceri broke the silence by announcing that she was fine with everything and they were not to worry about her. She then turned to David and announced, 'You've waited along time, and I'm sure you don't deserve it, but from now on I'm going to call you Dad.' David stared at her agog. He couldn't speak but got up and hugged his beloved daughter, his eyes brimming over with tears as were Beth's.

To break the emotional tension, Beth said, 'Let's go out and have a pizza.' They all agreed and Ceri turned to David, 'I hope you're paying Dad.'

'I can see you're starting as you mean to go on,' laughed David

'Too right!' she chuckled.

Ceri spent the next few days preparing for her Australian trip. Beth and David decided to spend some time in Cwn Rhedyn but before returning to Wales, the couple took their daughter to the airport at Heathrow. They waited until she disappeared through the gate. Beth told David that she felt as if her daughter was walking towards her future. David knew exactly what she meant and added he hoped things worked out for her and Steffan because he felt that they had that same special chemistry that he and Beth had. Beth nodded noting that she hoped they could have a proper life together quickly adding that she wasn't complaining because through it all, life had been good to her. David smiled and squeezed her arm and said with a smile,

'Pehaps we'll be grandparents yet.'

In bed that night, Beth turned to David and said,

'You know what this means don't you? Ceri will be going out to live in Australia.'

'You're getting a little ahead of yourself, love. Well if that's what she wants and if that's where her heart lies, good luck to her. There's always Skype and it's a great excuse for a trip Down Under. I can see us now strolling by the Harbour Bridge, walking up to the Opera house – perhaps even going in to watch a performance.' Beth nestled contentedly in his arms, loving his enthusiasm.

'Ceri is braver than me – she will probably go out there to her love. I was a coward. I was afraid to step into the unknown and follow you,' she sighed 'but I must stop thinking of the 'what ifs' and now live for the future - yours and mine' David kissed her gently at first and then made love to her passionately, showing her that they needed to make the most of this second chance.

They returned to London in time for Ceri's homecoming. She looked positively radiant as she ran to hug her parents at the airport. She was so excited and wanted to tell Beth and David everything about her wonderful trip. She had taken hundreds of photographs and although David had visited Sydney many times he loved re-living the experience through his daughter's eyes. Beth and David looked at one another and smiled,

'Well you certainly seemed to have had a wonderful time. We both wish you all the luck in the world, don't we Beth?'

Beth nodded and then spoilt the euphoria by mentioning the forthcoming Piers Morgan programme which was to be recorded in three weeks time. She and David were going to visit Anita the following week-end and they would then travel to Carmarthen to see David's mother Mrs. Meredith as David hadn't revealed the truth about Ceri when he visited her two days previously. Beth worried a lot about not telling Alun's mother and the more she mulled it over, the more aware she became of the need to inform her mother-in-law before the programme went out on air. After a long discussion with David about the matter, they decided to phone Alun's brother, Tony, and arrange to meet him in Carmarthen.

Anita was really pleased to see them both but couldn't make out why they were there together. She was taken aback when she was told the story and couldn't believe that Ceri was David's daughter although she had always believed he would have made a lovely father and was glad he now had that chance. She poured them all a brandy mainly because she felt she needed one and then mentioned the fact that her mother aught to be told. David nodded and said that they were on their way to Carmarthen after leaving her. Beth wasn't sure how Anita really felt about everything – she wasn't giving much away. The following morning the two women went for a walk together around Anita's vast garden. At first they hardly spoke but then Anita said,

'I can't get my head round the fact that you didn't confide in me Beth, especially as we had become such great friends.'

'That's exactly why I didn't. I didn't want you to think I was your friend just to get information about David. I became your friend because I really liked and appreciated your company.'

'I'm glad of that and yes, I can see your point. I'm not going to pretend that it hasn't been one hell of a shock but now I'm starting to get used to it, I'm really pleased for you both.' She gave Beth a big hug before returning to the house and doing the same to her brother. The meeting with David's mother was going to be rather tricky as both David and Beth were afraid to give her too much of a shock at her age but the old woman was far more astute than they had ever imagined. When she opened the door to them she didn't seem at all surprised to see them both there together. After the usual pleasantries Mrs Meredith said she was really glad to see them together at last. Beth and David glanced at one another,

'Don't look so surprised, I may be old but I'm not stupid. I've always sensed that sort of special relationship that you two have had over the years. I'm sorry you didn't get married when you were young but of course you must have had your reasons but there's nothing stopping you now, is there?' I'd like to see you happily married; my husband and I always had a soft spot for you Beth. We spoke about you often.' David hugged her but then told her that actually their past was a little more complicated than even she could have guessed. He told her the whole story whilst his mother continued to sit looking as elegant and composed as she always had.

'Goodness,' she said. 'I'm sure I shouldn't condone what you both have done but no doubt you had your motives, which are none of my business or anybody else's if it comes to that but people will talk and you must realise that some won't be too friendly towards you.'

'We know that,' said David, 'but as Beth mentioned the other day, the people who matter will still be there for us.' Mrs. Meredith stared out of the window and spoke quietly as if to herself, 'To think you had a daughter, David, and I a beautiful granddaughter all these years and I never knew.' A tear trickled down her still beautiful face. Her son went over and put his arm around her shoulder and she patted his hand and smiled. Beth slipped into the kitchen so that they could have some time alone together and managed to find everything to make them all a cup of tea. David's mother asked if she was to meet Ceri soon because although she knew her as Beth's daughter, she now had to get to know her as her own granddaughter before it was too late. Beth told her she would bring Ceri to Cwm Rhedyn soon and they would pay her a visit.

'Will you two get married?' she asked.

'We honestly don't know, Mam. The one thing we do know is that we will be together – I'm definitely not letting Beth get away again.'

'Well get married then,' she insisted, 'make an old woman happy.' They all laughed. Beth thought what a wonderful lady she was. How she wished that she could have had her as a mother-in-law instead of Mrs. Rees. That reminded her of the meeting they'd arranged with Alun's brother, Tony, the following day –how she dreaded it.

It was nice to sleep in their lovely room in Tŷ Cerrig that night. Carol had made sure the heating was on for them and there was a tasty casserole in the refrigerator ready to be re-heated. The morning came too soon for Beth's liking but they arrived in the lounge area of The Ivy Bush Hotel a little before Tony. Beth was very nervous about this discussion and she was right to be so. The first thing Tony said without even saying 'Hello', was,

'What's he doing here and why have you dragged me to meet you?' Beth thought that the best way to deal with him was not to beat around the bush and give it to him straight. She blurted out the whole story without taking a breath.

'Whoa!' said Tony, 'You mean to tell me that you were having it off with this bastard whilst you were married to my brother?' Beth nodded.'You tramp,' he shouted, 'you bloody bitch.' Everybody in the coffee lounge turned to stare at them and of course they all recognised David Meredith. David asked Tony to keep his voice down but was told to shut up. Beth wanted to run but she had to complete the job. When she told him about Ceri, he nearly hit the roof and for a moment Beth thought he was going to hit her.

'Why are you telling me all this sordid stuff now?'

'Because it's going to come out on Pierce Morgan's programme in the next couple of months. I thought it was better to tell you face-to-face.'

'My mother always said you were no good and Alun could have done much better. Poor Mam is going to be devastated.' He turned to David, 'To think how she loved your bastard as her granddaughter. It'll kill her. If it does, you'll have blood on your hands both of you.' Beth was shaking by this time and she could feel people's eyes staring at her. She desperately wanted to flee but David placed a steadying hand on her arm and calmly addressed Tony.

'Alun was a wonderful father to my child and I shall be eternally grateful to him. We are both sorry for a lot of things but we cannot change the past. What you tell your mother and the rest of the family is up to you but if and when they see the programme they can make up their own minds. Beth is not a bad person and was a very good, loving wife to Alun and Ceri loved her father very much and has always thought of you as her family. It is entirely up to you what you do about that relationship. I hope you can still think of her in the same way as she has no blame in this. I'm sure she'd like you all to continue as her father's family.'

Tony rose and said he'd heard enough for one day and just disappeared without another word, leaving Beth wondering what would happen next – would he tell his mother or not, and would they still stay in contact with Ceri?

'Take me home, David' she whispered. They drove to Cwm Rhedyn in silence because the meeting with Tony had upset them both in different ways. Beth couldn't settle – she didn't eat much all day and neither did she have much sleep that night. David heard her wandering about the house in the early hours of the morning but left her alone because he sensed that she needed to sort things out in her own mind. The following morning David announced that they should go back to London for the dust to settle and Beth made no objections as she was glad to escape. Soon after they had eaten breakfast and were getting ready to pack, the doorbell rang. When Beth opened it, she was faced with a crowd of journalists shouting questions at her. David came over to see what the commotion was about and was shocked to see what had transpired. A pushy woman from the local rag told them that they had had a phone call from a well-informed person and they, as the local newspaper, wanted to know if the report was true. Of course Beth and David knew straight away who had leaked the story to the press. Evidently Tony was going to play dirty. As always David took command of the situation by announcing,

'I don't know what you heard from your anonymous caller but let me inform you that I will be telling my life story on Pierce Morgan's television programme in a few weeks time. You'll get to know the truth then, and only then. Now, Mrs Rees and I are going to London to record that show, so you'll have to be patient. Thank you.' More questions were shouted at them but David closed the door firmly, hoping they would get the message and go away. Some left immediately but a few stragglers remained hoping for some titbits for their newspapers but were disappointed when they saw David and Beth drive away through the rear gates of the property.

'You were fantastic,' said Beth, 'How could you be so calm and yet so firm?'

'Years of practice, my love. Now let's try and forget everything for the time being. We'll stop for a nice lunch somewhere on the way, shall we?'

'That's fine by me' said Beth sleepily and as she dozed off, David glanced at her and smiled, thinking how good it was to be able to protect her.

Chapter 22

When they arrived back at the London apartment, a troubled Ceri was waiting for them.

'What's up, *cariad*,' asked Beth nervously.

'Uncle Tony's been on the phone – he was really horrible.'

'What did he say?'

'He called you and David all sorts of names and said I was nothing to his family any more.' She was crying as she continued, 'He said that *Mamgu* never wants to see me again. Do you think he meant it?'

'Probably he does at the moment,' said David. 'Let things be for a few days and then I think you should go to Swansea and confront them. After all nothing of this was your doing.' Beth agreed and gave her daughter a hug and told her not to worry, that everything would be alright but in her heart of hearts she wasn't quite so sure.

Before they had time to settle back in, a message came from the television company asking David to meet the production team and Pierce Morgan in three days time as they needed to record the programme the following week. 'Perhaps I should never have agreed to do this damned thing,' he stated. This time it was Beth who had to be strong.

'It has to be done, David, or we'll live a lie for the rest of our lives. Yes, we'll inevitably be a talking point for a while but people will soon get tired of our story and move on to other peoples' scandals. We must stay positive because we know we have each other and the love of people who care for us.' She turned to her daughter, 'Ceri, we are so sorry to have caused you so much pain, darling. I can't begin to forgive myself for that.' Ceri assured her mother that she was alright and to hell with all of them. If her father's family wanted to disown her, so be it.

The meeting with Pierce Morgan went well, both men realising that it would be a difficult interview as private facts were soon going to be public knowledge. Of course it was going to be a great achievement for the programme and especially for Pierce Morgan, himself but after the chat David felt reasonably confident that matters would be dealt with in a sensitive way. The day of the recording came very quickly and Beth felt sick as she accompanied David to the studio. Anita and Carol were going to be with her in the audience, which gave her a little more confidence. Both she and David had persuaded Ceri not to be present but she could watch the recording before they filmed her own clip.

'The interview opened with a general resume of David's career but they were soon on to the subject of Isabella and the divorce. David was asked why he had married her in the first place. He replied as honestly as he could, that his ex-wife was a very beautiful woman, they had a lot in common through their music and way of life and of course she gave him a lot of support with his career. Pierce Morgan asked if that meant she also had a lot of money to invest in him to which David had to reply, 'Yes.' It was mentioned that David had not said he loved her to which he replied that certainly he had loved her but not enough. He admired and respected her both as a person and as a singer and still did.

'Do you see her now? Pierce Morgan asked.

'We've met occasionally on the opera circuit, but we haven't worked together since we split up. We are however on speaking terms. The divorce was very amicable'

'Why were there were no children from the marriage?'

'Isabella was unable to have children and anyway our type of life wouldn't have been ideal for bringing up children.' Piers Morgan came in quickly and said,

'So you let another man bring up your only child?' The audience gasped. David tried to stay in control and Beth wore a pained look when the cameras focused on her. Carol held her hand tightly as David announced that everybody might as well hear the whole story. Piers Morgan related how David and Beth had been childhood sweethearts describing their lives before David went to college. There were a few snapshots of the two of them together for viewers to see. David was asked why Beth hadn't joined him in London. David tried to explain how things were very difficult as Beth was scared to leave her family at that time as her father was seriously ill. He clarified that she should have gone to college at Cardiff and he had never expected her to alter her plans for his dreams as that wouldn't have worked out. He described how Beth later took over the family business and made a great success of it. She met her husband, a local teacher and married him. He was asked if he still saw Beth during that time.

'Yes we met from time to time but we were both married by then. However there was always a special chemistry between us but we kept our emotions under control as we didn't want to hurt anybody.'

'Did you love her?'

'Always.'

'And her you?'

'Yes.'

'But you didn't give in to your feelings?'

'Not for many years.' Pierce Morgan asked him to clarify. David related the story about his sister's wedding and how they had slept together that night – for the first time, he added.

The interview continued. Pierce Morgan wanted to know what happened next. David told him about the baby and how Beth pretended it was Alun's and how thrilled he was at the prospect of fatherhood' as they'd been trying for a baby for years. Pierce Morgan wanted to know how David was so sure it was his.

'Can we just say that we knew?

'But how?'

Intimate details had to be revealed about Alun and Beth's marriage which made her feel very embarrassed.

'Why didn't Beth leave her husband at this point?'

'I was still married to Isabella and Beth wouldn't do anything to jeopardise my career. She didn't think my lifestyle was suitable for a young baby so she opted for a stable home and a doting father for her child. Alun was a brilliant dad and I'm very grateful for that' Beth felt a tear trickling down her face and as she wiped it away she was again caught on camera.

Pierce Morgan continued, 'I believe you were your own child's godfather? How did that come about?' David related the tale which sounded really far-fetched even to him.'

'Did it work out?'

'Yes, I think it did. I got to see my daughter and was able to develop a special relationship with her in my role as godfather. I was also able to buy her presents without anybody suspecting the truth and Alun had the child he'd always wanted.'

'Did anybody know the truth?'

'Only our dearest friend and confidant, Carol. She kept Beth sane over the years and was always there for her.'

'Did you and Beth manage to meet at all?'

'Yes, we had our moments.' Pierce Morgan and the audience laughed at this comment.

The interview was brought to a close with the story of Alun's untimely death and them revealing all to their daughter.

'Why the big reveal?'

'We felt it was the right time for Ceri to know and we hadn't hurt Alun by doing so.'

'Does your daughter accept you as her father?'

'It's been a very difficult period because it came as a great shock to her. These things take time but we're getting there. I'm very proud of Ceri and she knows that I would never try to take her father's place in her heart.

Beth has written her a series of letters explaining how things were and how we feel. She seems to have accepted our complicated relationship by now. She also has her own very successful career.'

'So life's turned out okay for you in the end?'

'Well I don't know what it's going to be like after this programme.' The audience laughed. 'It's taken a long time to get to where it is now but some things are worth waiting for.'

The interview concluded at this point. Most of the audience gave David, their hero, a standing ovation but Beth noticed that there were a few who remained seated and weren't even clapping. She supposed that was inevitable; David had let them down. The production team seemed very pleased and thanked David for his honesty. They said that they would be filming short clips with Carol, Anita and Ceri in the next couple of days and these would be slotted in to the programme at opportune moments.

Anita and Carol were staying with David, Beth and Ceri at the apartment until after the recordings. It would give David's sister a chance to talk and get to know Ceri as her niece. The whole experience had been very draining for all of them but they thought David had made a good job of a very difficult interview. The three short interviews were recorded in David's apartment. Carol was asked if she felt guilty about keeping her friends' secret for all those years to which she replied,

'It was a very difficult situation but I know that Beth would have done the same for me. Until now nobody has been hurt along the way and telling people at this stage was David and Beth's decision, not mine. These two should have always been together – they were soul mates but life becomes complicated sometimes. I'm glad that they have some time together now – I wish them all the happiness in the world.' Anita was asked if she knew what had been going on and she answered truthfully that she had no idea until a couple of weeks prior to the interview. She'd always sensed that David and Beth had a soft spot for one another but knew no more than that. She also mentioned that she was very pleased to know that Ceri was David's daughter as she'd been aware that Isabella couldn't give David any children. She added that her mother was thrilled with the situation as she'd always liked Beth. Ceri was very nervous but actually found the interview a vehicle to address Alun's family. She admitted that she was shocked and distressed when she was first told of the relationship between David and her mother but as time passed, and as she read her mother's letters, she became aware that life was not always straight-forward and people made compromises. Who was she or anyone else to criticise. She also said that through her own current relationship, she now realised how much David and Beth loved each other. Naturally she didn't mention her other relationship with Matt O'Conner and fortunately nobody seemed to be aware of it. Ceri carried on by saying the only concern she had was the loss of her father's family in all this as they had more or less disowned her. She wanted to send them a message saying that the deception had nothing to do with her and she would always think of Alun as her father, his brother, Tony, and his wife as her uncle and aunt and Alun's mother as her grandmother. She hoped that they could still find a small place for her in their hearts.

The programme went out on a Friday night. The following morning the telephone didn't stop ringing. The press wanted interviews but David said he had no more to tell them so it would be a complete waste of everybody's time and he informed the ones that tried to entice him with large sums of money that fortunately he didn't need their cash. Lots wanted to talk to Beth but David said, 'No,' so Beth kept a very low profile for the next few days. Carol and Anita returned to their respective homes, wondering what effects the interview would have on them. There were some derogatory comments on some of the social media sites but David just ignored them and tried to persuade Beth not to even read them – to no avail. Some of the remarks really upset her but she realised she'd have to be tough if she wanted to weather this storm. There were headlines in newspapers such as, 'The Secret Life of Britain's No. 1 Opera Star Revealed.' One good thing at least was that nothing had been added to what David had said in the programme. On the Sunday morning, Tony (Alun's brother) phoned Ceri saying that her *Mamgu* wished to talk to her. Mrs. Rees didn't beat about the bush. She said, 'You're no granddaughter of mine. How could you be such a turncoat, when your poor father loved you so much? How dare you live in the same house as that man? As for your mother – she's an evil, deceitful bitch. I never liked her and there she is swanning around in my son's house as if she deserves to live there. She's managed to ridicule my family and I shall never forgive her or that man for what they've done. I don't know how I'll face the neighbours.' Ceri didn't utter a word as she was so shocked. Tony grabbed the phone from his mother and added,

'You're not welcome here – we disown you and if you ever get married don't bother to send us an invitation to your wedding because we definitely won't be there.' He hung up and Ceri sat on the edge of her bed and wept. Beth was appalled when Ceri told her what had happened and had no real words of comfort for her. David suggested they'd come around given time. As it was going to be *Mamgu's* birthday soon, Beth suggested that Ceri send her a birthday card as usual. She said she'd give it a try but wasn't at all hopeful that things would get any better.

David and Beth decided to go to Cwm Rhedyn the following week to face the music. It would also give David an opportunity to see his mother again. They weren't sure how the villagers would react but they soon found out. On the whole it was a very frosty homecoming. Carol had already warned them that there was a lot of malicious gossip. When they took a walk down to the post office on their first morning back, many people snubbed them; many just came out and told them exactly how they felt but worst of all were the ones who whispered and sniggered behind their backs. Some of Beth's choir members had formed a deputation and visited her at Tŷ Cerrig. Their message was that the choir had decided that they would like to find another conductor. Beth was devastated by their reaction – after all what went on in her private life didn't affect her ability to conduct the choir. David told her that perhaps it would be wise to step down anyway. She could say that her reason for doing so wasn't anything to do with the recent revelations but she would be too busy doing other things and would not always be available for the choir when they needed her.

'But David, I love my choir and I've spent so much time getting them to their present standard. How could they be so nasty?' She was about to cry so David held her close and told her there were other things she could do in the music world.

'What?'

'Well now that I'm retired from the Opera circuit, I can still perform in one-off concerts so I'd like you to accompany me as you did at the very beginning. Would you do that for me?' Beth smiled and said,

'Of course I would – that would be lovely. I'd have to practise a lot.'

David replied that she'd been the best accompanist he'd ever had, probably because they understood each other so well.

'What if nobody asks you to sing after this fiasco?'

'I've got enough people all over the world more than willing to invite me to perform, don't you worry. They wouldn't care a damn about my private life. Imagine, we could travel the globe together as it always should have been.' This idea lifted Beth's spirits. She told David that she didn't feel that Tŷ Cerrig and Cwm Rhedyn were her home any more as she felt so betrayed by the people she'd grown up with. David knew how she felt but persuaded her not to make any rash decisions.

Decisions were actually made for them when they visited David's mother, that evening. They told her about the reception they'd had in Cwm Rhedyn and David added that although they had the beautiful apartment in London, they liked to be able to come back to their home area if and when they needed a break from city life. Mrs Meredith nodded, sat them down and said,

'I've been thinking. There is an alternative. You could come and live here with me.' David and Beth glanced at each other. 'I mean that I would have the summer chalet in the garden refurbished and live there, you could sell Tŷ Cerrig Beth and then pay out Anita's share of this house. Anita would have the money now rather than later, and the house would be yours and kept in the family. You'd be out of the immediate firing line and you'd also be doing me a great favour. This house with all its land is much too big for me to manage and I'd have some company nearby from time to time.' The couple didn't know what to say except that Beth admitted she had never really like Tŷ Cerrig anyway. Mrs. Meredith told them to think about it and if they were interested she'd ask Anita to come over to discuss things.

They talked and talked about Mrs. Meredith's proposition and the more they discussed it the more it made sense but Beth said that she'd have to have a word with Ceri before making any definite decisions. Ceri was enjoying her much needed day off when her mother got in touch. Beth related how horrible people had been in Cwm Rhedyn and how even the choir had turned against her.

'Well Mam, perhaps it's what you deserve. People appreciated Dad and they probably don't like what you've done to his memory, any more than I do. So what are you going to do about it?'

Beth told her about David's mother's offer. She was taken aback by her daughter's reaction.

'Do as you bloody well like- you always do. I've lost my father – granted that wasn't your fault but it is yours that I've lost my father's family. Now I'm going to lose the home I grew up in and am forced to adopt another father and another grandmother. I really don't care what the two of you do – I'm not going to be hurt by you any more.' She switched her phone off and Beth, who was much shaken, went in search of David to tell him what had happened. A few minutes into the conversation, Carol called to see how things were. She could see straight away that there was something amiss. When she heard what had taken place she had to add,

'Well Beth you were determined to open Pandora's Box and now you're suffering the consequences. Did you really think everything was going to be hunky-dory?'

Beth replied that everything was going so well with Ceri and she'd even wanted to call David, Dad, so why had she suddenly turned like this? David said nothing but Carol thought it was time to put her friend straight about a few things.

'Listen, Beth. Ceri feels that you are rearranging her whole life just to do what you feel is right. Remember, all her memories are here at Tŷ Cerrig and by moving away you would be taking them away from her. I'm sure she thinks she would be losing the last links with her father and in a way you would be abandoning him. Do you understand?'

'I suppose so but David's mother's offer makes sense.'

'To you maybe but possibly not to Ceri. She's had a lot of hard knocks in a short time. I think you should go back to London and sort this out before committing to anything.' David agreed, so after lunch they packed their bags once more and headed back to London, calling on Mrs. Meredith on the way to explain the situation.

They were both deep in thought during the journey and didn't say much until David announced that he had an idea.

'I've got enough money, so we could buy Anita's share of my mother's house, resulting in you not having to go back to Cwm Rhedyn. You, on the other hand could keep Tŷ Cerrig and possibly rent it out or you could even gift it to Ceri if you so wished.'

'But David that would mean you having to spend a lot of your money on me.'

'My darling Beth, nothing would give me more pleasure. I've waited all these years just to be able to do that.' Beth thought about his suggestion and decided she would like to keep the property and would let it out as a holiday let, so that any time Ceri would want to go there, it would be available for her. Beth also liked the idea of a small income of her own. The last thing she wanted was to be fully dependent on David. David also mentioned that they could plan and decorate his mother's house together so that it would become their family home. Beth could see all the positive sides of this argument and felt relieved that they had something definite to offer Ceri and hopefully get her back on side.

Chapter 23

The apartment was empty when they arrived back in Chelsea. Beth was relieved in a way because it gave her some thinking time before seeing her daughter. After David had made them both some coffee and arranged for a 'Take-away' to be delivered, she phoned Carol to tell her about the possible new ideas regarding Tŷ Cerrig. Carol surprised her by adding yet another suggestion to the mix. Carol felt that now she had retired perhaps she could buy Tŷ Cerrig and run it as a 'Bed and Breakfast' venture. The house would be ideal for that usage and it would give Carol something definite to do with her time and money from selling the catering business. She also added that there would always be room there for Ceri to come back any time she wanted – she'd even keep Ceri's bedroom as it was and would not use it as part of her business as there would be still ample rooms for letting plus the summer house in the garden which she aimed to convert into a chalet unit. Carol was always brimming with ideas and usually made a success of everything she undertook. She concluded by reminding Beth that she had nobody to inherit her money or property so she'd be leaving Tŷ Cerrig to Ceri anyway as her only, much–loved goddaughter. Beth didn't know what to say, so Carol sensing this announced she'd call her again in the morning for her decision. Beth really couldn't get her head round this recent proposal so she put it past David. He thought it was a marvellous solution but Beth remained wary.

They were in the middle of their meal when they heard Ceri arrive. She put her head round the door saying,

'You're back then?' She was about to go to her room when Beth called her saying they needed to talk.

'Do we have to now?' Ceri asked, 'I'm really tired.'

'I think so,' replied her mother.

Ceri came in sheepishly and apologised for her earlier outburst on the phone. She tried to explain why everything had suddenly become too much for her and showed her mother what had come through the post the previous day – it was the birthday card she had sent to *Mamgu*. It had been returned unopened.

'You see Mam, I'm starting to feel that I'm losing everybody and everything including my childhood home – it makes me feel vulnerable and somewhat in limbo.'

'Oh *cariad*, I really haven't thought enough about the effect all this is having on you, have I? I've been very selfish and I'm extremely sorry for that. Please try to forgive me. I can't make everything right but I have been thinking about the house. I really never liked Tŷ Cerrig very much – it was definitely your father's house and he loved it. In turn you loved it and still do because you have happy memories connected to it. After the reception David and I had in the village last week, I really don't feel I want to stay there again. On the other hand we both love our home area and that's why Mrs. Meredith's suggestion seemed to solve things but again I didn't take you into consideration. However I have a few options to put before you which do address your feelings.' She described the three options – giving the property to Ceri outright, keeping the house and letting it but making sure Ceri could use it whenever she liked and Carol's most recent offer including bequeathing the property to Ceri after Carol's death.

'Have a good think about them Ceri and when you're ready, we'll talk. Now go to bed, you look shattered. I'll also have a think about what we can do about that *Mamgu* of yours – I've a feeling Tony's behind it all.'

'Perhaps you're right Mam.' She came over and kissed her mother goodnight and turned to David and said,

'I suppose you'd better have one too,' so she kissed his cheek and went off to bed leaving her parents smiling at one another other. David squeezed Beth's hand and told her they'd get through it somehow and sort things out for Ceri.

When Carol phoned the following morning to see what Beth thought of her plan Beth remarked,

'I'm not against it Carol but for once, I'm letting Ceri have the final say.' Carol thought that was fair enough and said that she'd be eagerly waiting for any news. Ceri didn't mention the house for a few days and Beth was determined not to pester her. Ceri eventually announced her decision. She was going to go with Carol's suggestion which seemed to make a lot of sense. Carol was overjoyed so Beth said she would come to Cwm Rhedyn the following week in order to agree on an acceptable price and then set the wheels in motion. Beth told David that he could go ahead and let his mother know so that she could in turn contact Anita. Hopefully David's sister could come over when they were in Cwm Rhedyn the following week. Beth was so relieved. David hadn't realised how Ceri's reaction and that of the people of Cwm Rhedyn had affected her. After all she had lived in the village all her life and suddenly everybody seemed to have turned against her, forcing her to flee from the place. Her ties with the village wouldn't be completely broken if Carol bought Tŷ Cerrig. David thought that could be beneficial. He was quite excited about moving into his own childhood home. It was a beautiful Georgian house set in superb grounds. His mother had told him to do what he saw fit to the house and not to think he'd be hurting her feelings by changing things. This would be David and Beth's first home together and they were starting to plan the alterations to the property to make it their own. He kissed her with enthusiasm and as they were about to move into their bedroom Ceri came through and asked if she could accompany them to Cwm Rhedyn as she was due a couple of days off from work. She explained that she'd like to visit the house before Carol bought it and made any alterations. Her mother appreciated her request, telling Ceri that she thought it would be a good idea for her to have a long chat with Carol to put her mind at ease about the future.

Beth telephoned an Estate Agent in Carmarthen so that they could value the house as soon as she and David arrived in Cwm Rhedyn. She told Carol to do the same so that they could decide on a price which made them both happy. David's mother's house also needed to be valued so that Anita would have her fair share if she was willing for David and Beth to buy her out. When they arrived in Carmarthen the following week the first thing they did was to meet Anita and find out her reaction. Anita was more than willing to accept their proposal as she would naturally welcome the money and realised that the smaller unit would be ideal for her mother's needs. So the plans began to take shape. Firstly, they would upgrade the chalet to the highest specifications so that it would be both cosy and comfortable for Mrs. Meredith and in the meantime there were weeks of sorting out to be done before the move could take place. Beth was aware that she'd have to do the same in Tŷ Cerrig.

Carol and Beth came to an agreement on a fair price for the house so things began to move relatively quickly. Ceri was satisfied with Carol's plans especially that her room was going to remain untouched for the foreseeable future so that she could stay with Carol any time she wished. Beth asked her daughter if she would be willing to meet David's mother soon. Ceri wasn't sure about it at first but gave in and was glad she had done so because she and Mrs. Meredith hit it off immediately.

Everything was moving at an extraordinary pace with the house purchases but everybody on board formed a very happy team. They were all excited about their prospective new lives until one morning Beth's mobile phone rang. She could see it was from her Aunty Doreen's care home. She thought something had happened to her aunt but the member of staff said that her aunt had been trying to contact her for a few days because she had something she urgently needed to discuss with her. It sounded very intriguing so Beth promised to be there soon after lunch.

She found her aunt sitting by the window gazing into space.

'Are you alright, Aunty Doreen, you don't seem quite yourself. Are you ill?'

'No, no nothing like that.'

'Is it the news about David and myself? I'm sorry if it's upset you. We never meant to hurt anybody.'

'Yes it is partly about that.'

'Did you watch the programme?'

'No but people were more than willing to tell me all about it especially your cousins.'

'I'm so sorry Aunty Doreen, I don't know what you must think of me.'

Her aunt held tightly on to Beth's hand and told her the most shocking thing she could possibly have divulged.

'You know when I explained that I'd never tell you who your real father was, well due to recent circumstances I have to. How was I to know how serious you were about David Meredith. I thought you were just childhood friends – part of the same gang – you never told me he was your boyfriend.'

'No because I sensed that for some reason you didn't like him.'

'No it wasn't that. If I'd known the reality about your relationship, I would have stopped it. Your mother never spelt it out and when David Meredith left the area for greater things I didn't think any more about the two of you. You then married Alun and I naturally thought you'd broken all ties with the Meredith boy – Oh how wrong I've been and so stupid. That's why I have to tell you the truth now.' Beth started feeling very uncomfortable and wasn't sure if she wanted to hear any more but the old woman carried on.

'We were very young as I've already told you - Hywel Meredith and me. We made a mistake. I'd never have held him back from becoming the wonderful doctor that he was. I never mentioned that I was expecting his baby. Nobody was told who my baby's father was – not even your mother' Tears fell down Aunty Doreen's cheeks and Beth could feel her own blood run cold and she started to tremble as the enormity of the situation dawned on her. David's father was also hers – they were half brother and sister and David was Ceri's uncle as well as her blood father. Beth rose, tugged her hand away from Doreen's and ran to the nearest toilet and was violently sick. She started to cry uncontrollably resting against the sink. One of the care home staff found her there and tried to calm her down, asking if there was anything she could do to help but Beth just shook her head feeling defeated as she returned to her aunt before leaving.

'Why now,' she sobbed, 'now that we are so happy?'

'I'm so sorry Beth love – I should have told you earlier.'

'You should have but it's too late now. It's too late for everything. You should have kept it to yourself you stupid old woman. What the hell am I going to do – you've spoilt my life, David's, his mother's and our precious daughter's. How on earth can I tell them all this? We were all so happy this morning – planning for our future together but there is no future – not for my David and me. It's entirely your fault.' Beth collapsed in a heap on the bed and started to cry again. One of the care home staff brought her a cup of tea sensing that something major had happened to make Beth react this way. Beth took a few sips of the sweet tea and got up, saying she had to go. She didn't kiss her aunt as she usually did but fled down the corridor without a backward glance. It was the last time Doreen saw her daughter.

Beth drove her car erratically down the narrow roads towards Carmarthen. A few drivers tooted their horns at her because of her dangerous driving but she didn't stop. She skidded into the driveway of David's mother's house, left the car ignition on and raced up the stairs to the bedroom she shared with David. She knew he'd gone to arrange building quotes for the renovation work and Ceri was over with Carol, making plans. Beth heard David's mother call up to her but ignored her. Instead she found a scrap of paper and a pen and scribbled on it –'*My darling David, my one and only love. I'm so sorry but I can't go on any more – it's too horrible. I can't even bring myself to tell you what has happened but if you ever find out you will realise why I just can't live with it. The only person who can tell you the truth is my Aunty Doreen. You will not like what she has to say. It affects us all. I am a coward and am taking the easy way out. Forgive me. Remember I'll always love you.*

Beth.

The tears she shed dripped on to the paper, forcing the ink to smudge a little. She folded the note and placed it on David's pillow before running back to the car and driving off at break-neck speed.

Chapter 24

At the same time as David read Beth's letter, a local man, walking his dog, came across her body. The police later found her car down by the river in Cwm Rhedyn – near the spot where she and David used to walk when they were young. Beth had just waded into the swollen river and as she couldn't swim, found herself out of her depth very quickly. She simply let the strong current carry her away without a struggle. Her body was found about two hundred yards downstream.